101
STREAMS OF LIGHT
IN LIFE'S SOJOURN

101
STREAMS OF LIGHT
IN LIFE'S SOJOURN

Joy George
&
Varghese Gee

2018

101 Streams of Light in Life's Sojourn - Published by the Rev. Dr. Ashish Amos of the Indian Society for Promoting Christian Knowledge (ISPCK), Post Box 1585, Kashmere Gate, Delhi-110006.

© Authors, 2018

English translation of the original Malayalam Devotional *Jeevitha Vazhiyele 101 Prakasha Dharakal*

ISBN: 978-81-8465-676-3

Laser typeset by

ISPCK, Post Box 1585, 1654, Madarsa Road, Kashmere Gate, Delhi-110006 • *Tel:* 23866323

e-mail: ashish@ispck.org.in • ella@ispck.org.in
website: www.ispck.org.in

Preface

Christian writers, literary authors and publishers in Christian literature in India have given us the luxury of choice from among a large collection of devotional books and writings in English as well in almost all regional languages. Many of these are authored by scholars well-versed in theology, and many by those who have devoted their lives and time to the study of the Scriptures. There are also regular periodicals and daily devotional readings brought out by evangelical groups and houses anchored by biblical scholars. These efforts have undoubtedly enriched the spiritual lives of the Christian community and given many of them the courage and fortitude to meet the challenges in their lives.

This Devotional is of an entirely different genre and an innovative initiative. It has been authored by persons without any formal theological schooling who, while pursuing their professional vocations heard the "Still, Small Voice", and followed a divine calling and spread the word of God. This could be carried out only through their spiritually gifted motivation. The Devotional which does not attempt any scholastic interpretation sets itself apart in as much as the book catches the immediate attention, particularly of the youth, with its flowing narrative profusely interspersed with all-too- familiar verses from the Bible. Each chapter is so easy on the mind and intellect as if it is in conversation with the reader. Every episode with its personal message and appeal to the heart is bound to stay with the reader who is sure to come back to it, time and again, recalling and realizing that it is a positive adjunct in his attempt to attain the" Peace of mind that passes all understanding" and help the reader move forward, step-by-step in life's sojourn on earth.

This is an inspirational effort to act as a catalyst in the spiritual upliftment of the readers. The overall thematic message of the book is Christ's all-embracing love towards humanity for whose sins He made the ultimate Sacrifice on the Cross.

Joy George

Varghese Gee

❖ 1 ❖

Father, I have sinned against heaven, and against you. I am no more worthy to be called your Son.

Luke 15:21

From the beginning of creation, God granted man and woman the freedom to choose and the power to discern. This led to humanity's first sin committed by Eve and Adam through the evil design of Satan in the guise of a snake.

In the parable of the 'Lost Son' we come across three different facets of humanity. There is the father, the personification of love and affection; the foolish and misguided son wanting to lead a life of pleasure and profligacy; and the self-seeking elder son apparently having every reason to be upset at the family assets being divided. Let us have a look at the role of each of the three in this parable.

Each of the first two has exercised his freedom of choice asserting his will in his own way to suit himself, whereas the ever-loving father even without a second thought gave away the share of the younger son - an example as to how God never stands in the way of our freedom of choice.

And the elder son? From an outsider's point of view, his stand would appear to be justified. "Let this demanding and ill-advised brother be out of the way", he would have reasoned. That is the reason why he was angry when his brother, who frittered away all his share of the family wealth, returned and would not be pacified by the father.

The younger son took his share and left to "squander his wealth in wild living" (vs.13) away from the benevolent control of the father. Realisation dawned upon him that the pleasure-seeking life was just a mirage that left him in ruin, hunger (he was not allowed to fill his stomach even with the pods that the pigs were eating (vs.16) and friendless. He decided to go back fully confident that his loving father will forgive him. What the remorseful son tells his father is the key verse here (vs.21). The loving father, who might have spent sleepless nights ever since his son walked out, forgives and re-claims him with open arms. This gives a vivid picture of the new life that a loving and forgiving God offers to a sinner who repents and returns to him. Repentance and the attendant catharsis enables each sinner to come back into the Father's fold.

The Father's approach to the enraged elder son is particularly noteworthy. "My son you are always with me and everything I have is yours" (vs.31). The gospel does not mention whether this sulking son joined in the celebration arranged, by the father for the return of the 'Lost Son'.

Let us introspect to find where we stand between these two sons. Are we like the prodigal son who squandered the father's wealth but returned to him in full repentance. Or like the unrelenting elder son who refuses to be reconciled. Let us, be fully conscious of our sins, come back into the path of repentance and remorse, seeking the Father's forgiveness and the ever loving and forgiving Father, will take us with open arms.

"If we confess our sins, he is faithful and just and will forgive us our sins and purify us from all unrighteousness' – 1 John 1:9.

❖ 2 ❖

If you falter in times of trouble, how small is your strength?

Proverbs 24:10

Here we are faced with an inalterable truth, that this life on earth is full of trials and tribulations. Only their degree varies with individuals. How do we face these and go through them? For one whose faith is anchored in God, each crisis is a challenge and a step forward in life's onward journey. The propelling factor is one's unshakable belief that the one in whom he has reposed his faith, is always with him as a guiding star. God has never promised us an easy passage in our sojourn on earth. On the contrary, there is challenge as well as comfort when we are told "In this world you shall have trouble. But take heart, I have overcome the world" (John 16:33).

Listen to what the psalmist says "Cast your cares on the Lord and he will sustain you, he will never let the righteous fall" (Psalm 55:22). In other words, the Lord gives us the strength and fortitude to bear any burden and move forward.

Think of the utter disbelief of the eaglets when the eagle stirs up her nest. The little ones do not know the mother is preparing to teach them to face life so that they can soar higher and higher in the sky against the worst windy storms. When God tests us during the most unexpected times we must realize that he is preparing us for greater things which our limited faculties are unable to comprehend.

During his days on earth, while going through the most difficult and testing times, at the Mount of Olives "He withdrew about a stone's throw away from the disciples and prayed on his knees "Father, if you are willing, take this cup from me (Luke 22;42). Simultaneously subjecting himself unconditionally to the Father's will.

So, when our faith is tested during the most trying times, let us dedicate and subject ourselves to the Almighty's plans for us with renewed faith in the one who has guided and cared for us so far.

"Rejoice that you participate in the sufferings of Christ, so that you may be overjoyed when his glory is revealed" – 1 Peter 4:13.

❖ 3 ❖

Unless the Lord builds the house, its builders labour in vain and the Lord watches over the city, the watchmen stand guard in vain.

Psalm 127:1

Our life on this earth is a tight rope walk. Often, we live on the razor's edge. For all things under the sun, there is a measured value and a balancing effect, which if upset, will lead to our downfall. It is God who controls these within his finely defined parameters.

For the faithful one, there is always a plus factor with him, all the twenty-four hours of the day. In arithmetical notation + God. This is what should give us a mindset leading to the thought that it is I and my God today, tomorrow and for all days to come.

Let us have a look at the passages in the Bible which are relevant to this thought. When we are chosen to attempt great things for God, His voice resonates in our mind in the same tenor He spoke to Jacob. "So, do not fear, for I am with you (Isaiah 41:10). And God strengthens Joshua when he proclaimed "Have I not commanded you? Be strong and courageous. Do not be terrified; do not be discouraged, for the Lord your God will be with you where ever you go. (Joshua 1:9). After he rose from the dead, Jesus assured his disciples "And surely I am with you always to the very end of the age (Matthew 28:20). And the disciples are thus empowered to preach his kingdom to all nations on earth. In all our endeavour, great or small, our God is always with us, strengthening and guiding us through every step.

It is the same concept that the psalmist reiterates in the key verse of Psalm 127 quoted as the leading verse in this note. Home, clothing and food are the basic needs of any human being. The psalmist touches upon only one such need, namely 'home', in the first part of the verse. He underscores here the 'plus' factor without which the builder's efforts are in vain. The second part of the verse incorporates everything else, our life as well as our material possessions. The watchman who stands guard is portrayed as the plus factor. In other words, God must be with me and on my side in everything I do. At the same time, we are not to be boastful about God being on our side, as Abraham Lincoln famously puts it "I do not boast that God is on my side, I humbly pray that I am on God's side. This is what you have to ensure in everything we do, from the first to the very last." I am Alpha and Omega, the Beginning and the End, the First and Last (Revelation 22:13) in all things great and small.

Dear friend, all our efforts where God's presence is absent is in vain and fruitless. It should be God and I in everything, let us remind ourselves, every hour of the day and night.

"Trust in the Lord with all your heart and lean not on your own understanding" – Proverbs 3:5.

❖ 4 ❖

When words are many, sin is not absent, but he who holds his tongue, is wise.

Proverbs 10:19

"Silence is golden". Solomon's words amplify and dwell on this age-old pearl of wisdom. When our tongue runs ahead of thoughts, our thinking gets initiated unintentionally. That is why a man of few words is seen as a wise one in Solomon's eyes.

Our society often looks down upon someone who is quiet and prone to listen in silence to conversation what takes place around him. Such a person is even dubbed as a smooth wily operator who keeps all the cards close to his chest. This is a reality that we often come across in many groups which find indirect pleasure in indulging in gossips and even character assassination behind someone's back. Those with measured words are always suspect and one who takes a principled stand, while others indulge in their own fun seeking activities in a group are branded as unsocial.

Avoid commenting about a third person in conversations. It so happens that another person listening does not take it in the right spirit and this will likely to be interpreted as gossip. Therefore, we should realise the importance of Solomon's words "He who holds his tongue is wise". By gossiping and spreading rumour about others we are only demeaning ourselves and sinning in the eyes of God. Is it not wiser and safer to be branded as 'DUMBO' in Society? Think it over.

Let us take heed of what James says. "Everyone should be quick to listen, slow to speak and slow to become angry" (James 1:19) Psalmist compliments this teaching when he affirms "I will watch my ways and keep my tongue from sin. I will put a muzzle on my mouth as long as the wicked are in my presence" (Psalms 39:1). Let us put these into practice in our daily life. Let us examine ourselves and see that a congenial atmosphere is created even when a few of us are gathered. Pray to God to give us strength and will to correct ourselves and lead us along the path of righteousness.

"Wives are to be women worthy of respect, not malicious talkers but temperate and trustworthy in everything" – 1 Timothy 3:11.

✤ 5 ✤

Yet to all who received him,
to those who believed in his name,
he gave the right to become children of God.

John 1:12

The earth and all universe are the creation of God. Christ came into this world to save humankind but the world neither recognized him nor accepted the fact that God had sent His only begotten Son for the salvation of humankind. In the key verse above. John asserts that whoever receives and believes in him is given the unique position and power as the Children of God.

Those who believe in God must be doers of God's will. Only then they are eligible to be called the children of God. They have certain designated positions as well as rights. Just as in worldly affairs children must sub serve a father's will and be obedient to him to inherit his earthly possessions, we also must subject ourselves to the will of God to be partakers in his Kingdom. If we examine today's family structure, we find a world of difference between the old and new generations and the reasons for the same are many. Especially in a joint family, comprising father, mother, sons and daughters and their spouses and grandchildren, it is natural to have misunderstandings based on flimsy grounds. Instead of jumping to conclusions which often prove baseless, what is required is to talk things over among the concerned individuals. Such an open approach could easily dispel any unfounded suspicions and misgivings. Each one in the family should have the courage to take such an initiative to maintain the peace and tranquility that should permeate a blessed family.

Sri. T. Padmanabhan, the noted writer brings out certain touching scenes in his story titled "Father and Sons" which are quite relevant to the present-day family atmosphere prevalent. The children seek reasons to ignore their parents. Let all concerned individuals take time to talk things over and we can reduce the flow of our old parents to old age homes.

Dear friends: Is this how we repay our parents who sacrificed their all to bring us up to our present position. What they need at the fag end of their lives is a little care, love and company from their loved ones. Think it over. Let our conscience give us the answer. Remember,

"How great is the love the Father lavished on us that we should be called the children of God" – 1 John 3:1.

❖ 6 ❖

My lips will not speak wickedness, and my tongue will utter no deceit.

Job 27:4

These are the words uttered by Job swearing by the name of the Almighty who caused him unbearable mental agony and physical and material suffering.

What this verse underscores are Job's unalterable faith in God. Despite unexpected and unbearable personal losses - loss of health, loss of children brought up with care and love, and all that he cherished - Job was not prepared to disown God. Even in such trying circumstances he was resolute in his faith in the creator. He even overcame the isolation brought about by his friends and declared that he would not speak against the Almighty "So long as I have life within me and the breath of God in my nostrils". This shows Job's faith firmly grounded in God and he contemptuously dismissed even his wife's exhortation to deny the existence of God. What was the net result of his absolute faith in God? God gave back to Job many fold and blessed him in far greater measure than in the past.

Dear friends do not forget that Satan first threw a challenge at God before setting up himself on Job to test him. The same evil force is after us even today all the time. Let us be on our guard constantly. Eternal vigilance is a prerequisite to meet and defeat temptation that Satan brings to us. When we face trials and sufferings, there could be external forces which are bent upon testing our faith. But to overcome these we should be in communication with God through constant prayer to give us strength and unflinching faith in him and above all for his grace which makes us sufficient in everything. These will take us forward through the worst of times with confidence. Peter reasons us by saying,

"Your enemy the devil prowls around like a roaming lion looking for someone to devour" – 1 Peter 5:8.

Let us therefore be on our guard all the time.

❖ 7 ❖

The eternal God is your refuge and underneath are the everlasting arms.

Deuteronomy 33:27

These are part of the pronouncements made to the Israelites by Moses, the man of God, before his death.

He takes them over the wonderful ways in which God has guided them all along, the crossing of the Red Sea and the innumerable instances when the Almighty "rode on the Heavens to help them and on the clouds in His Majesty" (vs.26).

Strong arms beneath us always gives us assurance and strength like children feeling secure in their mother's arms. Our God is our father and mother and we are his children. If we believe so, should not the fact that the everlasting arms underneath us, gives us comfort, confidence and courage? Let us meditate upon this verse when we are confronted with life's trials and tribulations, and it will give us an inexplicable inner strength and self-confidence to face them. This is also what the psalmist says when he assures that "God is our refuge and strength, an ever-present help in trouble" (Psalm 46:1).

He further reassures "It is God who arms me with strength and makes my way perfect (Psalm 18:32).

Christ assures us "even the very hairs in your head are all numbered, so don't be afraid (Matthew 10:30, 31). What better and solid promise do we need from our God, even though the sinners do not deserve any of His Grace? Therefore, dear friends, even if we find our future dark and uncertain, let us take comfort and confidence in the knowledge and belief that the "everlasting arms are under us". Be of good courage.

❖ 8 ❖

Honour your father and your mother.

Mark 7:10

It is a common saying that childhood is life's foundations and old age its roof – a comparison to a home and how it has been built up over a period starting with a foundation and completing with a roof. When we take a family, parents are its foundation as well as its roof, children being its pillars of strength.

In course of time, if the pillars get weak, the structure itself collapses. Is this not the state of affairs of many families today, even forcing authorities to bring in legislations to protect the elderly?

This reminds me of a family consisting of father, mother and two children – a boy and a girl. Their worldly possession is just a piece of property inherited by the father. The father, with his meager income from an ordinary job, educates the children to the best of his abilities. Within their limited means, the parents managed to ensure that their son gets a reasonable job, and the daughter happily married off assuring at the same time to keep intact, whatever they have inherited. They secured the future of the children while tightening their own belts.

In the meantime, the son gets married and seeing the extravagant life style of the son and his wife, the father cautions them, reminding the son of the difficult days, his parents went through to bring the children up to the position where they are now. And the son's stone hearted reply "This is inherited assets and what has been your contributions" went like a sword through the father's heart, bringing tears down his cheeks. Is not this anecdote, a true reflection of the mindset of the new generation? The words of Solomon – Son, take heed of my words and preserve my teaching like the ball of your eye – should make the present generation sit and introspect. They should follow and adhere to his advice that a wise son needs to heed to his father's advice. It is high time that they realise the sacrifices rendered by their parents, for the sake of children, without, at the same time compromising the dignity of the family.

Youngsters should take pride, that they are following the ways of God shown to them by the elders and make it an article of honour to care and be considerate to them, thereby setting an example to others. Never forget that your treasures are "in heaven" where neither moth nor rust does corrupt and where thieves do not break through nor steal", for where your treasure is, there will your heart be also". (Matthew 6:20-21). Caring and sharing for the elderly is undoubtedly such a treasure.

❖ 9 ❖

These Commands are a lamp, this teaching is a light, and the corrections of discipline are the way to life.

Proverbs 6:23

The sixth chapter of proverbs opens with the exhortation "My Son". Through the subsequent verses, the son is called upon to follow the instructions of the father, and not let go the mother's advice. Father, mother, son – these three individuals together constitute a home. A home that is rooted in God, is the longing and blessing of any believer. Each constituent of this trio has its own role designated by God.

Children are parent's hope and expectations. Instructions of the father are guiding stars to the children and lights to lead them away from darkness and the mother's advice an alluding comfort. Light and comfort together is a blessed combination in one's journey through this dark and troublesome world.

"In his epistle to Timothy, what the apostle Paul underlines, is noteworthy. He (that is the head of the family who acts as the overseer) must manage his own family well and see that his children obey him with proper respect" (1 Timothy 3:4).

What is required as complimentary to these qualities is underlined by the apostle in his advice to fathers.

"Fathers' do not exasperate your children; instead bring them up in the training and instruction of the Lord (Ephesians 6:4).

Solomon in the proverbs brings out another dimension to the father - son relationship. "He who spares the rod hates his son but he who loves him is careful to discipline him" (Proverbs 13:24).

There is no denying the fact that children should be punished, when the occasion demands, taking care at the same not to hurt their feelings. In modern day times when corporate punishment from which ever quarters, could turn out to be an offence under the law, parents should fall back upon the power of prayer, counsel their children to walk in the path of righteousness and grow up in the grace of God. And the almighty God who never fails us, will no doubt answer our petitions and prayers, with the desired results.

❖ 10 ❖

I have fought the good fight, I have finished the race. I have kept the faith.

2 Timothy 4:7

Today's key verse given above is a part of the letter written by apostle Paul while he was in jail for the second time. The letter was written to Timothy, his helper and "Son" (Paul addresses him in Ch. 1:2 as Timothy my dear Son). The apostle exhorts Timothy to carry forward the work he has been doing.

The apostle charges Timothy with the task of spreading the word of God at the beginning of the chapter – "I give you this charge; preach the word; be prepared in season and out of season; correct, rebuke and encourage with great patience and careful instructions" (vs.2) adding at the same time, how he himself began and now ending this mission, by his unshakable faith in God. The same advice he extends to the Church in Corinth. "Do you know that in a race, all the runners run, but only one gets the prize." (1 Corinthians 9:24).

Just as a runner should not run aimlessly, so also should we not take the gospel lightly. Therefore "do not run like a man running aimlessly; do not fight like a man beating the air" (1 Corinthians 9:26). So, with a firm resolve, we should be partners in the gospel mission, to obtain the crown. Each Christian should strive to be a missionary all to himself / herself. As Paul challenges Timothy "Endure hardship with us like a good soldier of Christ Jesus." (2 Timothy 2:3). As part of his missionary work, apostle Paul's life was one full of misery including various forms of physical torture. He asserts while like an athlete competing in a race, "he does not receive the victor's crown unless he competes according to the rules." (2 Timothy 2:5). He compares a battlefield and racing track as similar, in as much as the goal in both endeavours is victory.

Where ever we have been placed by God, whichever is the area of work assigned to us by him – that is our arena for the battle or the track for race. And the all-knowing – omnipresent God, decides who the victor is. Simultaneously, let us assess ourselves whether we have performed enough and are worthy to win. Let us pray to God to give us the grace to go forward in the strength of Christ to receive the victor's trophy. "One thing I do, forgetting what is behind and striving toward, what is ahead, I press on towards the goal to win the prize which God has called me heavenward in Christ Jesus." (Philippines 3:13-14).

❖ 11 ❖

That is what the Lord says. Do not go up to fight against your brothers, the Israelites. Go home, every one of you, for this is my doing.

1 Kings 12:24

This is a part of God's instruction to King Rehoboam through prophet Shemaiah to whom he appears in a vision. Shemaiah tells the king that it is God's will that Rehoboam should not go into battle against the Israelites. God forbids them from the battle and the king and his advisors realise what is God's will and they go back. We find here that any move against God's will, will be blocked by him.

Where ever we try to go against the divine purpose, God places an obstacle by his own chosen methods. We came across such instances throughout the Bible. Jonah tries to defy God's will but is prevented by means that we find extra ordinary (Jonah chapters 1 & 2).

The magi was deputed by King Herod to Bethlehem to look for the child Jesus with his own hidden agenda. But the magi, having been warned by God in a dream returned by taking another route avoiding Herod (Matthew 2:7-12).

At the same time God also creates opportunities to fulfill His will. One such example is found in 1 Kings, chapter 17. God sends prophet Elijah to the widow in Zarephath, which ultimately leads to the widow and her family being provided with their daily material requirements of food and other needs for the rest of their lives.

Let us listen to what the Psalmist says. "You know when I sit and when I rise, you perceive my thoughts from afar, you discern my going out and my lying down (Psalm 139.2-3). In all things concerning us, whether big or small, do we not find divine hands of God guiding us? What comfort it gives, above all what peace it provides? "Peace I leave with you my peace I give you. I do not give to you as the world give. Do not let your heart be troubled and do not be afraid" (John 14:27).

❖ 12 ❖

When the woman saw that the fruit of the tree was good for food and pleasing to the eye, and also desirable for wisdom, she took some and ate it.

Genesis 3:6

Recently I came across a question raised regarding creation – why did God wait till the last day to create man? The answer to the question was also given alongside - to create best of all creations. "God created man in His own image; in the image of God, He created him; male and female, He created them" (Genesis 1:27).

A creation totally different from other creations, because God gave human the wisdom to discern, the freedom to choose. And Satan capitalised and took advantage of these unique characteristics of human. Look at the way Satan tempts Eve. "The fruit of the tree was good and pleasing to the eye and also desirable for gaining wisdom" (Genesis 3:6). What else does one need? And this is the first drop of poison that Satan injected into the woman's mind and successfully deceived her.

Satan tempted even Christ and not just for one moment or a day but for forty successive days as we read in Luke, chapter 4. Satan's calculation was that someone who fasted for forty days at a stretch could be an easy prey. But Jesus chose to defeat him using God's words" (Luke 4:1-12).

Let us always be on our guard against the clever ways in which Satan tempts us by playing on our desires. Eve falls for her desire and thereby Satan successfully plants the seed of sin in her, which led man to his first act of disobedience to God. God gave his first punishment by throwing Adam and Eve out of the garden when they gained the knowledge of discerning good and evil. And thus, came the ever-continuing misery for the entire humankind.

Dear reader! Are we leading a life of rebellion against God? Are we falling into the trap laid by Satan by falling for what is "pleasing to the eye and tasteful for our palates"? Are we disobedient to God? When you are tempted, you cannot take the plea that you are being tempted by God. Each one falls for temptation because of his/her desires and search for earthly pleasures. Sin is born out from lusts of our flesh, fulfilling the desires of the flesh and of the mind. This is what led to the downfall of Eve and then Adam. Just like the angler uses a small fish to catch the big fish, so is Satan capitalising on our material desires and pleasures of the flesh. Therefore, put on the full armour of God so that you can take your stand against the devil's schemes (Ephesians 6:11).

✤ 13 ✤

Stay there until I tell you.

Matthew 2:13

The angel of the Lord appeared to Joseph in a dream and gives him the above instruction. Joseph is asked to take the child Jesus and the mother and escape to Egypt. And God wills that they stay there till he is told to do so and Joseph submits himself to the will of God. If we look at our own lives, whatever happens to each one of us, when and how long, is a divine decision. Illustrations for these are plenty throughout the Bible.

An angel of the Lord tells Philip – "Go south to the road… the desert road… (Acts 8:26). We should note here that Philip is directed by God not to take an easy and comfortable path, but a 'desert road' which is a traveller's nightmare. Philip obeys, and, on the way, he meets an Ethiopian eunuch, an important official in the court of the Ethiopian queen and it turns out to be a life changing event in the Ethiopian's life, when Philip baptizes him. And look at the way God opens sight and a new vision for Saul who "breathed out murderous threats against the Lord's disciples and transforms him into a chosen instrument to carry His name before the Gentiles and their kings and before the people of Israel" (Acts chap. 9). Here is a zealot and fanatic who carried with him the SEAL of authority from the high priests to take the Lord's disciples as prisoners is touched by God and thereafter is driven with the ZEAL and passion of the divine spirit. Likewise, we come across many children of God beginning with Abraham, who left everything and got moving once God had called them out.

God called Albert Schweitzer: He left his job at the university, learned and mastered the scriptures and theology and went to spread the word of God in Africa. God has thus a divine purpose for each one of us. Wherever we are called out and wherever we are placed, even if it is a displacement from a comfortable zone , put your faith in God, trusting that there is a divine hand behind it. Give glory to the one who has called you and take up the task assigned to you with joy. The Lord God, who was with Abraham, Issac, Jacob, Moses and all our fathers and guided and guarded them in his mysterious ways, will also be with you and will turn you into a useful and purposeful instrument in his hands. Have faith in his calling and in his hands that will always be around you to keep you from falling.

Remember "As for God, his way is perfect, the word of the Lord is flawless. He is a shield for all who take refuge in him". Psalms 18:30.

❖ 14 ❖

Whoever can be trusted with very little can also be trusted with much, and whoever is dishonest with very little, will also be dishonest with much.

Luke 16:10

This is part of a parable, Christ told his disciples to highlight the Pharisee's greed and love for money. What is 'integrity', which has many dimensions? This is a quality required in every walk of life - wealth, character, work culture and above all, our relationship with God. We recall various anecdotes to teach our children, the need to learn this quality even when they are young, so that they can put it into practice, all through their lives – wherever they are placed and in whatever circumstances they find themselves.

There was Stephanose who was faithful to God to the very last even when he was martyred for his belief in Christ. We have sterling examples in our own time, like Sadhu Kochukunju, the ever faithful and gifted carrier of God's words. Any one lesser in faith could not have composed such a courageous song at the time of the passing away of his son, when he wrote those soul-stirring lines saying that he will still sing praises 'Halleluiah' to God even if he is handed the cup of sorrow from which he will drink with joy. Let us read this along with the words of Christ at Gethsemane. "You do not know what you are asking, can you drink the cup I am going to drink? he asks his disciples (Matthew 20:22) and 'My Father if it is possible, may this cup be taken from me, yet not as I will, but as you will" (Matthew 26:39). What we read in chapter 39 of the book of Genesis is exemplary of the integrity of character, shown by Joseph. On the other hand, Ananias and Sapphira in Acts chapter, 5 personify deceit and deception when it came to wealth.

We find that the basic reasons for such acts of unfaithfulness is a lifestyle where there is total lack of integrity and urge for righteousness. Let us therefore, try to create a conducive situation starting with our own homes. Even in day to day dealings are we true to ourselves even in such small things when the telephone rings and the children are told to respond negatively? If we are not faithful in such little things, how do we expect God to entrust us with bigger tasks. Are we not deceiving ourselves when we practice deceit in our own homes? So, let us guard ourselves so that we do not fall into greater sins and invite the wrath of God.

Even in our work places, especially in educational institutions where children are moulded for the future, there is lack of sincerity and seriousness. It is even more disturbing when this is carried out by those who are supposed to be role models for the youth. Though we call ourselves "Christians", are we not Christians in name only and no different from the pharisees mentioned by Christ? Do we practice what Christ has called upon us to do and fall on the path shown by him? Let us pray to God to give us the strength and courage to be Christ-like in our thoughts, words and deeds, thereby setting an example to others.

Above all, let us be true to ourselves in everything. "Truthful lips endure forever, but a lying tongue lasts only for a moment" – Proverbs 12:19.

❖ 15 ❖

Blessed are the pure in heart,
for they will see God.

Matthew 5:8

Purity is always measured as an essential element in all walks of life. All of us, women in particular are only too familiar with 916, the measure with which purity of gold is evaluated. But in a person what is to be assessed is the purity of his/her heart. Sometimes this is not considered as a point of strength; but a characteristic more often mistaken for incompetence. We often label such a person as ineffective and incapable. But purity of heart is a solid source of strength when combined with righteousness. Such a person has always the courage of conviction and will never compromise on his principles and can face any body or any situation without fear of consequences.

This is also what Christ taught through his sermon on the mount. Before spelling out what the Beatitudes are, "he went upon a mountain side and sat down.... and began to teach them (Matthew 5:1-2). "Blessed are the pure in heart, for they shall see God". This is our key message here.

Let us read this along with the others who are blessed, those "poor in spirit" – the meek – the merciful – peace makers", all qualities complimenting to purity of heart". Such people approach God courageously because they stand for what is right. They fear only God and no one else.

When we grow in God and in his words, we are transformed into persons with purity of heart. When little children were brought to

Jesus, for him to place his hands on them and pray for them, the disciples rebuked those who brought them. And Jesus responded by teaching the disciples some simple home truths". Let the little children come to me, and do not hinder them for the kingdom of Heaven belongs to such as these" (Matthew 19:14). Jesus made the disciples understand that those who have the innocence of children and "the purity of their hearts", have free access to God, all the time. And the Psalmist extols the same virtue, when he says that only those whose walk is blameless and who does what is righteous, who speaks the truth from his heart and has no slander on his tongue will dwell in the sanctuary of the Lord (Psalm 15). So, let us try to live a clean and pure life, doing only what is right and seeking God's help to achieve this through constant prayer.

"Blessed are they whose ways are blameless who walk according to the law of the Lord. Blessed are they who keep his statutes and seek him with all their heart" - Psalm 119:1, 2.

Let us keep this always in mind.

❖ 16 ❖

I could not do anything of my own accord, good or bad, to go beyond the command of the Lord – and I must say only what the Lord says.

Numbers 24:13

We, who are believers in Christ are to lead a life based on his commandments. Those who do not believe in the Lord and do not allude by his directions will never be a blessed lot. This is the sum and substance of the message contained in the book of Numbers.

Balaam was summoned by Balack to curse his enemies, the Israelites. But when the spirit of God came upon Balaam, he instead blessed the Israelites through his third oracle "May those who bless you be blessed and those who curse you be cursed" (vs.9). On hearing this Balack's anger burned against Balaam. Balaam firmly stood by what the Lord had commanded him to do as is seen in our key verse given above. "Even if Balack gave me his palace filled with silver and gold, I could not do anything on my accord, good or bad, to go beyond the command of the Lord (vs.13).

Let us contrast this with what is happening around us in modern times of materialism, which should make us sit up and think. Instead of being satisfied with what we have and learning to live within our means, we try to compete with others, who show off their wealth. What is the resultant effect? We run into debts and fall into the traps of "Loan Sharks" and ruin not only our lives, but also that of our near and dear ones. Balaam is a shining example of one who refuses to be tempted by greed.

Every household should make it a point to account for each paise it spends. These days, the new generation do not even like to be questioned as to how they spend what they acquire. We should not forget that whatever material possessions we have is only a trust entrusted to us by God which has to be spent judiciously and justly in the sight of God.

In modern times, "gratification presents" and "under the table payments" are an accepted way to "facilitate" things and get one's job done. One should not forget that such methods are not only corrupt and abominable in the sight of our Lord, but also denial of justice to those who are upright and deserving. It is for each one of us to decide, whether we should be satisfied once our bare needs are met and not our greed. The dividing line between need and greed is very thin and will ultimately decide whether we value peace of mind over everything else. There is nothing more precious than peace, the peace promised by Christ "Peace I leave with you, my peace I give unto you not as the world gives" (John 14:27). Let us always walk in the path of truth as apostle John puts it, "I have no greater joy than to hear my children are walking with truth" (3 John 4).

❖ 17 ❖

Always pray and not give up.

Luke 18:1

While Jesus has elaborated upon the various aspects of prayer from time to time, here Christ brings out another side - the need for constant prayer. To underline his advice to his disciples the need to "pray without giving up" Jesus tells the parable of the persistent widow who by her sheer persistence, forces a judge to give her justice. The lesson he taught through the parable was that God will answer the prayer of those who constantly plead with him day and night.

After Jesus taught his disciples how to pray, he told the story of a person who goes to his friend in the middle of the night for help, to further illustrate the strength of prayer. Here Jesus tells how the 'boldness' of the person forced his friend to give in (Luke 11:5-9). That is also what we are told in Hebrews 4:16. "Let us then approach the throne of grace with boldness and confidence. In 1 Thessalonians 5:16, apostle Paul calls upon us not only 'to pray continually' but also at the same time 'to be joyful always' and 'give thanks in all circumstances'. That is when God will hear our cry with the assurance "Never will I leave you; never will I forsake you" (Hebrews 13:5).

But one thing we should understand. There is no time limit for the response to our prayers. We cannot be waiting for a reply like we are expecting for a letter after posting it. We do not know when our prayers will be answered. May be sooner, may be later. There could be delay but never denial. God will answer our prayers according to his scheme of things He has prepared for each one of us. And God expects as never to be doubting Thomas. Be patient and wait on the Lord, "Though it lingers wait for it; it will certainly come and will not delay" (Habakkuk 2:3). So, let us learn from the hardworking ant and the spider who taught Robert Bruce the need to be patient and never to be disheartened or give up. Let us therefore keep in mind our Lord's words to "Always pray and never give up" and approach his throne of grace with the confidence that the one who has heard our prayers in the past will answer them in the future as well.

"Ask and it will be given to you; seek and you will find, knock and the door will be opened to you" - Luke 11:9.

❖ 18 ❖

As I have loved you, so you must love one another.

John 13:34

Here Jesus teaches his disciples what ought to be the measure of love. First, he gives a new command "Love one another". Then he shows them in what manner and how deep love should be. Jesus also reminds them that only if they love one another, they can claim to be his disciples.

Love is the central theme that runs through the holy scriptures. When an expert on the law stood up and tested Jesus with the questions as to what he should do to inherit eternal life, Jesus meets him with a counter question and forces him to answer as per the law in which the questioner himself was supposed to be an expert. "Love the Lord your God, with all your heart and with all your soul and with all your strength and with all your mind and love your neighbor as yourself" (Luke 10:27). Then Jesus tells the law expert to go and live as per the law himself. But to test Jesus further, the law expert then asks Jesus to show him who his neighbour is. Could there have been a better way of defining a neighbor than the story of the good Samaritan, which Jesus illustrated through example and put the law expert to silence (Luke 10:20-37).

There cannot be a better description of love than what is set out at length by apostle Paul in chapter 13 of 1st Cor., which is a 'Celebration of Love'. Even before he begins the chapter, the apostle says, "And now I will show you the most excellent way". The Bible has many examples of those who have been tested and yet remained steadfast in love. Let us listen to what Ruth had to say to Naomi "where you die I will die and there I will be buried. May the Lord deal with me be it ever so severely, if anything but death separates you and me" (Ruth 1:17). And the love of Mary Magdalene, who stood outside the tomb of Jesus, crying (John 20:11).

When Jesus told his disciples to love one another, what he meant was unconditional love, irrespective of personalities involved and the circumstances in which we are and never expecting anything in return. Christ demonstrates such love in all its purity, when he, the Lord and Teacher, washed the feet of his disciples. When he told them "I have set you an example that you should do as I have done for you" (John 13:15), he was also calling upon each one of us to follow that example of how to love one another as well as one's neighbor. "And now these three remain faith, hope and love. But the greatest of these is love" - 1 Corinthians 13:13.

Dear friend! Always bear in mind these words of Paul.

❖ 19 ❖

Do not fear, for I am with you, do not be dismayed, for I am your God.

Isaiah 41:10

This message is an inseparable part of the very existence of a believer. A belief that there is the powerful hand of the Almighty in all the right things we do gives us the strength to go forward. This is what gave Shadrach, Meshach and Abednego, had the confidence to tell king Nebuchadnezzar. "If we are thrown into the blazing furnace, the God we serve is able to save us from it and he will rescue us from your hand" (Daniel 3:17).

When Peter and John stood before the Sanhedrin and spoke with authority the word of God, the priests and the captains of the temple were taken aback. Even more so, when they realized that both Peter and John were unschooled ordinary men (Acts Ch.4). God's words of courage to Joshua, gave him the confidence to lead the Israelites even after the death of Moses. Paul calls upon Timothy to shake off his difference because "God did not give us a spirit of timidity, but a spirit of power, love and of self-discipline" (2 Timothy 1:7).

My friends in Christ, let us look back and do an introspection to examine in what areas of our life, we have left things undone, where it ought to have been done at the appropriate time, and what were the reasons behind our failures. Let us during the time given to us in our journey through this earth, put our trust in God and go ahead with the task entrusted to us. His mighty hands are always beneath us lest we fall.

Let us say "The Lord is with me I will not be afraid, what can man do to me" - Psalm 118:6.

❖ 20 ❖

Carry each other's burdens and in this way you will fulfill the law of Christ.

Galatians 6:2

If we examine the context in which apostle Paul's epistle to the Galatians was written, we will realize that the Church in Galatia comprised entirely of non-Jewish Christians. Paul explains to them that it is through faith in God and not through the observance of law, that we are counted as righteous in the sight of God. He also exhorts them to preserve the gifts they have received through grace.

Paul gives this advice as a remedy to avoid the pitfalls one comes across in daily life. Therefore, he wants those who are spiritual, to restore someone caught up in sin without giving any room for themselves to be tempted (Gal. 6:1). Throughout Christ's teachings we find the importance he gives to love, kindness and the need to help each other. These qualities are essential if we are to carry each other's burdens. The very foundation of this is love. That is why Apostle Paul calls upon us in Romans 15:1 "We who are strong ought to bear with, the failings of the weak". And Christ teaches us to love others even our enemies unconditionally. "Love your enemies, do good to those who hate you, bless those who curse you, pray for those who mistreat you" (Luke 6:27-28).

When we talk about someone's burden, it includes all that causes mental agony and physical disabilities to that person. Here what the apostle underlines is the "mental burdens" of a person, since the apostle is linking it to the law of Moses and the Old Testament. As such the most important quality needed for us to bear one another burden, is love.

My friends in Christ remember that Jesus bore all our sins, the heaviest burden, on the Cross for us sinners. Once we learn to love each other without any reservation we will be able to lighten the burden of others by sharing and caring for them. We should pray to God to give us the grace to carry forward this mission entrusted to us by him.

Always remember "The fruit of the spirit is love, joy, peace, patience, kindness, goodness faithfulness, gentleness and self-control. Against such things there is no law" - Galatians 5:22-23.

❖ 21 ❖

The Spirit told Philip
"go to that chariot and stay near it."

Acts 8:29

A typical example of how God uses his children to fulfill his purpose of accomplishing his task in this world, is given in the key-verse above.

Let us have a look at the situation when this call came to Philip. After Stephen's martyrdom, great persecution broke out against the church at Jerusalem. All except the apostles were scattered throughout Judea and Samaria. Those who had been scattered, preached the Word of God wherever they went. Philip went down to a city in Samaria and proclaimed the Christ there. The crowds heard Philip and many sick were healed. It is recorded that there was great joy in the city (vs.8). Philip preached the good news of the kingdom of God and baptized both man and woman. It was there that the angel of the Lord directed Philip to go to Jerusalem (vs.26). Everything had been planned and chartered by our Lord. It was there on the desert road to Gaza, the angel of the Lord directed Philip to go near the chariot and he simply obeyed.

There he met an unexpected personality, an important official - a powerful minister of the Queen of the Ethiopians. At his request, Philip travels with the Ethiopian and interprets to him the portions of the scripture and the good news about Jesus. The Ethiopian got baptized and proceeded happily. Philip was directed by God for another mission.

This is only one example of how God makes his children fulfill his missions. We find in the Bible many stories where believers were taken to work in unexpected ways by God. We are only coworkers with God, to serve his mission in this world.

We find the Lord appearing to Ananias and directing him to Saul (Acts: 9:10-17). Saul gets back his eye sight. He was baptized. Saul was transformed and became eventually Apostle Paul. Abraham, Samuel, Jonah and Elisha, all of them are God's children called by God to accomplish certain missions.

We find instances in the Bible where God restricts Paul and Bernabas from preaching in the province of Asia.

Dear friends! Have not we also experienced such things in our daily life? When our plans to take up a covetable job, thwarted, did we not really get very much upset over that and later when we found civil war broke out at these places, did we not really thank God for blocking us from going there.

Remember, our Lord has, plans and missions for every one of us. All we must do is to listen patiently to the call of our God.

See how the Lord used Moses "Now go, I am sending you to Pharaoh to bring my people the Israelites out of Egypt" - Exodus 3:10

❖ 22 ❖

Wait for the Lord be strong and take heart and wait for the Lord.

Psalms 27:14

This is the last verse in this psalm of David. If we read through the first few verses, we find that David had his own apprehension that a civil war would break out at any time. And he says "Though an army besiege me, my heart will not fear, though war break out against me, even then will I be confident. (vs.3) David's staunch belief in his Lord is clear from this statement.

Dear friend! Can we with confidence uphold this statement? We should, and we can. For that, what we need is strong confidence in God and the belief that nothing is impossible with God and if God is with us who can be against us. Bear in mind the words of Apostle Paul. "I can do everything through him who gives me strength" (Philippians 4:13).

One essential characteristic of a believer in Christ is strong courage. A father and son walking along the road in the thick of night, find the street lights are off suddenly. A natural question of a father to the son "Are you afraid". The son's instant reply "Not at all. You are with me". This should be the relation between a believer and his God. The essential difference between fear and courage is 'fear' is what we ask for, while 'courage' is what we build up with the grace of God. The strong belief that God, the Almighty is with us all day and night should be our watchword. This is what David means when he says in our key-verse "Wait for the Lord... Even though I walk through the valley of the shadow of death, I will fear no evil for you are with me" (Psalm 23:4). This brings out the same meaning.

Be strong in the Lord whom our forefathers believed and who taught us to hold strongly to our belief in the Lord under all circumstances. Let the words of the apostle "persecutions, sufferings, what kind of things happened to me…, the persecutions I endured, yet the Lord rescued me from all of them" (2 Timothy 3:11, 12) give us courage and strength to follow Christ and his teachings.

Let us boldly shout "In you, O Lord, I have taken courage, let me never be put to shame" (Psalm 71:1).

❖ 23 ❖

The Lord said to Ananias, Go! This man is my chosen instrument to carry my name before the gentiles and their kings and before the people of Israel.

Acts 9:15

Saul was breathing out murderous threats against the Lord's disciples and was on his way to Damascus with letters from the high priests to take persons who follow Christ's way, as prisoners to Jerusalem.

It was then that Saul was called by Jesus and he fell on the ground and was blinded.

Those with him, led him by the hand to Damascus and for three days he was blind and could not eat or drink anything. At that time the Lord called Ananias in a vision and gave him directions as given in our key verse.

Our Lord had chosen Saul for his work and Ananias was deputed to make Saul God's chosen instrument to preach the gospel of the Lord among the gentles and their kings and before the people of Israel. Ananias met Saul and placed his hands on him and proclaimed to Saul that the Lord Jesus (who appeared to him) had sent him that he might see again. Immediately Saul got his eyesight back. He was baptized and we find him staying with the disciples in Damascus and he began to preach that Jesus is the Son of God. 'Saul grew more and more powerful and baffled the Jews living in Damascus (vs.22). One thing we must understand clearly here is that God can convert any sinner and use him for God's desired purposes, to enable him to declare "I have been crucified with Christ and I no longer live but Christ lives in me" (Galatians 2:20). Only after his conversion, Saul did realize that Jesus Christ will forgive our sins and redeem us.

Dear friend! Let us pray to God to forgive our sins and strengthen us in his grace. Our almighty God who forgave Saul (who was a threat to the Church and the disciples) and Peter (who denied Christ), will take us into his fold to become trustworthy soldiers of Christ.

❖ 24 ❖

Daniel resolved not to defile himself.

Daniel 1:8

Daniel and his friends Shadrach, Meshach and Abednego were captives brought from Jerusalem to Babylonia. They were brought to the palace and had been put on duty to serve the king. We find these youngsters very keen in not doing anything against the wishes of the God, whom they served. They were determined to obey God according to the Law of Moses and they resolved not to defile themselves with the royal food and wine. They requested the chief official in charge of them to exempt them from taking the royal food. God had caused the official to show favour and sympathy to Daniel and we find them being allowed to take vegetables and water instead of the royal food. The Lord was with them and gave knowledge and understanding of all kinds of literature and learning. "The king finds none equal to them" (vs.19).

Here let us bear in mind that during the royal surroundings they kept true faith in their God. It is recorded that "three times a day he got down on his knees and prayed giving thanks to his God first as he had done before (Daniel 6:10) and as such all of them prayed to God regularly, three times a day and that gave them courage and strength not to do anything against their God's will.

In our present day set up, many youngsters leave their homes to faraway places like Daniel and his friends. What best we, at home can do is to remind them to follow the examples of Daniel and his friends and pray to God daily. At the same time, let us pray to God to give them strength and courage to refrain from doing anything that will defile them under any circumstances.

❖ 25 ❖

God is faithful, he will not let you to be tempted beyond what you can bear. But when you are tempted he will also provide a way out so that you can stand up under it.

1 Corinthians 10:13

Paul in his letter addressed to Christians in Corinthians in chapter 10 begins with a reminder of the history of their forefathers. And later in the text, he advises them to avoid setting their hearts on evil things. Added to the bits of advice, he encouraged and strengthens them as stated in our key verse.

From the very beginning of the creation Satan, our principal enemy, is after us to keep us under his control and our only weapon to escape from his clutches is to keep constant association with our Lord through prayer. "The Lord is near to all who call on him, to all who call on him in truth" (Psalm 145:18). In such a situation the devil could not do anything except to retreat. See what our Lord Jesus Christ did. "Do not put the Lord your God to test" (Luke 4:12), he told the devil and the devil retreated accepting defeat. Our prayer "Lead us not into temptation" which Jesus had taught us will act as a shield to combat Satan and his evil intentions. We find Peter becoming a prey to temptation and disowning Jesus Christ. He went outside and wept bitterly (a sign of repentance). Almighty God forgave his sins and took him back into his fold. He spent the rest of his life for the Lord God and died a martyr. Paul from his own experience gives an advice in our key verse. He affirms that, had it not been for Christ's resurrection, he would never have been able to undergo such sufferings and thus have fellowship with Christ sufferings "Flogged more severely and been exposed to death again and again" (2 Corinthians 11:23). But he kept his faith and for Christ's sake delighted in weakness, in insults, in hardships, in hostility and hatred. Dear friends! believe firmly that our God will not let us be tempted beyond what we can bear and when tempted, we always have a powerful weapon "prayer" to combat it. Remember what Christ had said to his disciples at Mount Olives "Get up and pray so that you will not fall into temptation" (Luke 22:46) and let us pray "Lead us not into temptation but deliver us from the evil one" (Matthew 6:13).

❖ 26 ❖

The same Lord is Lord of all and richly blesses all who call on him.

Romans 10:12

A postle Paul in Romans Chapter 10 deals mainly with salvation. "If you confess with your mouth "Jesus is Lord" and believe in your heart that God raised him from the dead, you will be saved" (vs.9). Salvation is a gift, provided if one has faith and expresses it as a witness to others. Resurrection is undoubtedly the foundation of our Christian faith. A true Christian believes that Jesus Christ died on the cross for our sins and was resurrected on the third day and that the Lord still lives. Peter and John and others saw the risen Lord. But to many others, the living Lord is a matter of faith. To a believer Jesus died for our sins and is still living. That is faith. In other words, believing is a matter of faith which God alone can see and judge. The message in the key verse reiterates that those who trust in him and call on him will be richly blessed and it says that "everyone who calls on the name of the Lord will be saved" (vs.13).

Irrespective of caste or creed, God the Almighty will richly bless those who believe and call on Him. And we should always bear in mind that one must believe in God and his promises and request him who is always ready to accept our plea and supply abundantly. "But when you ask, you must believe and not doubt, (James 1:6)." See what Bartimaeus, the blind man did. He began to shout, "Jesus son of David have mercy on me" (Mark 10:47). Jesus replied "Go, your faith has healed you" (Mark 10:52). The blind man got his sight and Jesus richly blessed him. The absolute faith of the Canaanite woman got her daughter's freedom from demon possession. Jesus certified "woman you have great faith" (Matthew 15:21-28).

Secondly, we must do the will of God.

"Not everyone who says to me 'Lord, Lord', will enter the Kingdom of heaven but only he who does the will of my Father who is in heaven" (Matthew 7:21). Only good trees will bear good fruits.

Dear friend, don't you want to hear Christ's voice "well done my child, you have great faith". Then believe in God and do His will. Please understand that "to all who received him, to those who believed in his name, he gave the right to become children of God" (John 1:12).

❖ 27 ❖

Were not our hearts burning within us while he talked with us on the road and opened the scriptures to us?

Luke 24:32

Our message for thought given above is part of the conversation between two disciples of Christ, on Easter afternoon during their journey from Jerusalem to Emmaus, a village, seven miles away. They were returning from the tomb of Christ and were discussing the happenings of that morning reported to them by Mary Magdalene, Joanna, Mary the mother of James, and the others with them. It was then that a third person joined them and took part in their conversation. Apparently, the disciples did not recognize Jesus. "They were kept from recognizing him" (vs.16). They narrated the happenings from crucifixion to resurrection. Both felt something unusual in a stranger expounding the scriptures. "He explained to them what was said in all the scriptures concerning himself" (vs.27). We find Jesus staying with them at their bidding. "When he was at the table with them, he took bread, gave thanks, broke it and began to give them" (vs.30). Then their eyes opened, they recognized him, and he disappeared.

Let us for a moment examine ourselves. How many of us sincerely wish Jesus' company and look for an opportunity to invite him for dinner with us? Do we not also sometimes get a feeling, of our hearts burning within ourselves? "Jesus himself came up and walked along with them" (vs.15). But they did not recognize Jesus. If we ponder deeply, it can be said that in many instances we do not realize or recognize the presence of our Lord near us, although our hearts burn within us.

Never hesitate to entertain visitors. "By so doing some people have entertained angels without knowing it" (Hebrews 13:2).

Jesus' words "whatever you did for one of the least of these brothers of mine you did for me" (Matthew 25:40). "Whatever you did not do for one of the least of these, you did not do for me" (Matthew 25:45). Dear friend! Bear in mind always these words of Jesus.

❖ 28 ❖

Everything comes from you, and we have given you only what comes from your hand.

1 Chronicles 29:14

David became the King of Israel. He defeated the enemies of Israel and united them into a powerful nation. David, later called the assembly and while praising the Lord in the presence of all the members, he spoke the words given as our message for thought.

Have we ever taken time to think of this verse? How true is this statement? This is a question addressed to each one of us. Let our conscience answer.

David proclaims, "All these things have I given willingly and with honest intent". Like David, let us be able to vouch safe, that, what we give to God is with whole hearted sincerity and utmost pleasure".

A classic example of giving to God with pleasure is narrated in the Bible – the story of the boy with five loaves and two small fish (John 6:15-13). When Jesus looked up and saw a great crowd, he told the disciples, to provide food for them, and it was then Andrew, brother of Simon Peter spoke up "Here is a boy with five small barley loaves and two small fish". We find Jesus feeding the five thousand, with these five loaves and two fish. Perhaps, this boy heard about Jesus and the miraculous signs he had performed on the sick, wanted to see him and came with Andrews and Peter. No details are given about this boy, anywhere in the Bible. Surely, his mother might have packed some food for him. We see, here, the boy giving the packed food very willingly to Jesus (through Andrews). This boy giving with pleasure everything he had, to Jesus, resulted in several people being fed happily to their full.

Giving to God with conditions like "a chicken to the Church if all the eggs hatch", is not what our God expects from us, his children.

In other words, entrust what little we have, to Jesus like the boy with five loaves and two fish, and he will multiply and feed many to their full satisfaction.

Dear friend! "If your enemy is hungry give him food to eat, if he is thirsty give him water to drink" (Proverbs 25:21).

❖ 29 ❖

The Lord is good, a refuge in times of trouble, He cares for those who trust in him.

Nahum 1:7

The people of Nineveh turned from their evil ways, through Jonah and "God had compassion and did not bring upon them the destruction he had threatened" (Jonah 3:10). God loved them enough to warn them, but the people of Nineveh repented temporarily and very soon they went to the black days they were in before. By Nahum's time there was no more Jonah, to turn them from evil.

The prophet Nahum during narrating his vision concerning Nineveh, he singled out certain statements about the Lord making known his anger against Nineveh "The Lord will not leave the guilty unpunished" (vs.3).

The key verse in our text is a part of his vision about the Lord.

Three important aspects are pointed out here and we find that these ideas are presented all along in the psalms. "Taste and see that the Lord is good; blessed is the man who takes refuge in him" (Psalm 34:8). "The Lord preserves the faithful" (Psalm 31:23).

"God is our refuge and strength, an ever-present help in trouble" (Psalm 46:1). "Call upon me in the day of trouble, I will deliver you" (Psalm 50:15).

"It is better to take refuge in the Lord than to trust in princes" (Psalm 118:8). Again, the Psalmist exhorts. "Those who seek the Lord, lack no good things" (Psalm 34:10).

"At an important stage in the life of David, he was in great trouble and "was greatly disturbed". But David found strength in the Lord his God" (1 Samuel 30:6). We find David inquiring to the Lord "will I overtake the raiding party" (1 Sam. 30:7) and at the behest of the Lord, he took courage and defeated the Amalekites. We know that the Lord cares for those who trust him.

Nahum in his vision makes clear that the "Lord is slow to anger and great in power; the Lord will not leave the guilty unpunished" (vs.3).

Dear friend! Let us admit our faults and repent. Pray to God, to give us grace to keep ourselves away from all inequity. Always keep in mind that "The Lord is a refuge for the oppressed a strong hold in times of trouble" - Psalm 9:9.

❖ 30 ❖

Whom shall I send? Who will go for us?

Isaiah 6:8

After the death of King Uzziah, his subjects were desperate and in turmoil. It was at this juncture Isaiah gets the vision when he heard the voice of the Lord. What the Lord said in that voice is the key verse given above. Isaiah took up the challenge and said, "Here I am, send me" (vs.8). And he took up the duty of informing the people what God communicated to him in the vision.

When we go through the rest of the verses, here we can understand one thing clearly. Only when our guilt is taken away and our sins atoned for (vs.7), will God entrust us with the task of carrying out God's mission.

Please remember that the vision of our forefathers and the call from above, enabled them to build up our valuable evangelical associations. E. Stanley Jones was called by our Lord to go to India, and as a result he came to India after completing his studies and consequently many knew and followed Jesus Christ.

Dear friend! Our Lord Jesus Christ wants each one of us to witness for him. Are we willing, is a long-standing question to us from Christ? It is high time for us to think over this.

"Commit your way to the Lord, trust in him and he will do this". Psalm 37:5

❖ 31 ❖

I am the Lord who heals you.

Exodus 15:26

Moses led the Israelites from the bondage of Pharaoh and the Egyptians. Our key verse is the promise God gave Moses on this occasion. 'You' in this verse covers the whole community which Moses led and 'heal' refers to the welfare of the people, their health, their mental attitude and the living conditions of the land they live in. Behind this promise the Lord puts certain conditions as well. They must listen to God and obey His commands.

The Lord provided what they needed. The bitter water of Marah became sweet when Moses put a piece of wood (as per the direction of the Lord to Moses). God promised the Israelites comfort, health, happiness and peace, if the commands of the Lord were taken care of. Throughout the Bible we find such a promise by God to those who obey the Lord's commands.

We find God appear to Solomon and assert "if my people who are called by my name, will humble themselves and pray and seek my face and turn from their wicked ways, then will I hear from heaven and will forgive their sin and will heal their land (2 Chronicles 7:14). Watch the condition the Lord puts before them "pray and seek my face and turn from their wicked ways". To Jeremiah, the Lord declares "I will restore you to health and heal your wounds" (Jeremiah 30:17). See how Jesus transformed Zacchaeus, the Chief Tax Collector to an entirely new person. He gave up his old life style and salvation was given to his whole house (Luke 19:9). What happened to the crippled woman whom Jesus healed? Let us examine the questions Jesus asked the synagogue ruler. Should not this woman, a daughter of Abraham, whom Satan had kept bound for eighteen long years, be set free on the Sabbath day (Luke 13:16). Jesus cured the demon possessed man (Luke 8:28-39).

Here we find the Lord who gives complete cure, to mind, body and soul. To this God, let us surrender ourselves and do His will, faithfully and completely and may the Almighty help us.

Dear friend! Can we with confidence say "I have set the Lord always before me, because he is at my right hand, I will not be shaken" - Psalm 16:8.

❖ 32 ❖

Trust in the Lord with all your heart and lean not on your own understanding.

Proverbs 3:5

Our father in heaven is aware of all our needs, God expects us to put before Him all our requirements and move forward with full faith and confidence in Him. Here we must bear in mind wise Solomon's words. Don't stress on 'Self' when we approach the Lord. Always take God along with us. In other words, keep in mind always – "God is with us" and with God we can do all things. Think what happened to Jonah in the book of Jonah. He gave all importance to his own feelings and deviated from what

God wanted him to do. This resulted in his being thrown into the sea and caught in the belly of a big fish. There he cried out to God for mercy. Mind, that all God's plans are worked through us only. Let us allow Him to accomplish his plans through us and He will work wonders.

This is what we read throughout the Bible. Psalmist reiterates this fact in Psalm 37. "Commit your way to the Lord, trust in him and he will do this" (vs.5).

Trusting fully in our God, without being proud of our own strength, do honestly the duties entrusted to us. God the Almighty will never forsake us.

Dear friend! "Trust in Him at all times pour out our hearts to Him, for God is our refuge" - Psalm 62:8.

❖ 33 ❖

Stop doubting and believe.

John 20:27

When the disciples were together in a room with doors locked fearing the Jews, Jesus appeared to them for the second time.

There Jesus pointing to Thomas said these verses taken as our message for thought. To these words Jesus added "Because you have seen me, you have believed, blessed are those who have not seen and yet have believed" (vs.29). Let us have a look at what is said in our Bible about faith. "Faith is being sure of what we hope for and certain of what we do not see" (Hebrews 11:1). We read, of Moses, Sarah, Noah, Abraham strong advocates of faith in the living God who all lived and died in faith having seen the promise afar off. Keep in mind what Jesus told the crowd "if you have faith as small as a mustard seed, you can say to this mountain, 'Move from here to there' and it will move" (Matthew 17:20). What did Peter do? Jesus directed him to throw his net into the deep; he obeyed resulting in getting a big catch (Luke 5:5, 6). Don't forget, how Jesus was tempted by Satan and finally left him at an opportune time.

In our struggle in this worldly life amongst pain and all sorts of sufferings the living God will hold us and take us safely to the other bank.

Dear friend! Pray to God who shares our sorrows and joys, who knows and sees everything and the Lord who 'watches over your coming and going' (Psalm 121:8) and "discern my going out and my lying down" (Psalm 139:3) will reward you in heaven. Is it not what we call "faith" by a child of God?

Please remember that "Blessed are those who have not seen and yet have believed" - John 20:29.

❖ 34 ❖

Gave... each according to his ability.

Matthew 25:15

In this parable (Matthew 25:14-30) Jesus reminds us of many truths. The gifts we receive from our God are very precious. Make sure that we use, God given talents to the best of our ability, and let us not be branded as lazy and wicked like the servant who had hidden his master's money in the ground. Instead let us make best use of intelligence, money, health etc. for the good of the community according to God's plans. Let God the Almighty address us as "good and faithful servants". Let us not underestimate ourselves and shy away from our duties. Our God will treat such persons only like the servant who hid his talents to serve no purpose. Jesus strongly condemns this sin of omission because it is more insidious than sins of commission, giving a sense of security and does not make us repent. Without admitting our failures and defects let us not put the blame on others and get, self-satisfaction. This was what the lazy servant in the parable did.

Our Lord does not expect this sort of an attitude from his children.

Dear friend! "Whatever you do, work at it with all your heart, as working for the Lord, not for men" - Colossians 3:23

❖ 35 ❖

And who is my neighbor?

Luke 10:29

To justify himself, one gentleman, an expert in law asked Jesus Christ this question (given as our message for thought) . If we go through the next few verses in the Bible (vs.30-39) we find Jesus answering this question by narrating a simple incident. A man was going from Jerusalem to Jericho when he fell into the hands of robbers. They robbed him and left him half dead. A priest, one Levite (assistant to the priest; that is usually said of him) all passed by this wounded man, self-satisfied with their own reasons for not attending this half dead man. Quite different to this approach, a Samaritan who passed that way attended to him, and cleaned his wounds and took care of him. Here we find the expert in law answering the question which he had put to Jesus "Who is my neighbor ", Jesus directed him to "go and do likewise" (vs.37).

Dear friends! Here is a question to all of us. How many of us can go an extra mile to become a friend like this? Think it over; have we not at one time or another given up this opportunity to become a friend. Our Lord Christ wants us to make use of such occasions and be generous in giving time, money and love to the man in need and become a 'friend'. Pray to God to make us a 'good Samaritan'. Please remember that.

"A friend loves at all times, and a brother is born for adversity" - Proverbs 17:17.

❖ 36 ❖

As for me and my household, we will serve the Lord.

Joshua 24:15

We read in our Holy Bible how Joshua led the Israelites with the full support and blessing of the Lord. He defeated all their enemies and brought peace to Israel. At the fag end of his career, we find him directing the Israelites to assemble in Shechem.

The key verse for our thought is a part of the announcement he made to them. This Bible verse is invariably found on the walls of many Christian homes. The modern family set up normally comprises of father, mother and children. But still there exists many families with father, mother, children, grandchildren and grandparents living together. Whatever may be the circumstance when we say "me and my household we will serve the Lord" the first step inevitably should be to have daily family prayers in our homes. This is a traditional Christian family concept followed by our forefathers. A question we must ask ourselves is "How many of us follow our Christian tradition in its complete meaning and concept". Do we, in our homes adjust the prayer timings to suit the elders? I mean, the grandparents, if any, in the family. I remember in my younger days, we all, including full time servants, sat around a mat for family prayers. This is one of the primary duties of Ammamar (mothers) in the family. For a well-knit Christian family, a peaceful atmosphere of love and mutual trust is inevitable. Jesus' command "Love one another" (John 13:34), also "pleasant it is when brothers live together in unity" (Psalm 133:1). To achieve this and to make it solid, family prayers play a very important role. God is always present when two or three assemble for prayer together. This will find an answer to all our ills and problems. Absence of regular family prayers can be accounted for the increase in family breakup in our Christian family set up these days.

Let us faithfully serve our God, as a family to give absolute meaning to the Bible verse in our homes. Pray together, share our pains and problems as one family. This will surely make our family set up more solid and pleasant. Remember, love and loving one another is the urgent need for the present world set up. For that, love should begin from our homes.

Listen, my son, to your father's instruction and do not forsake your mother's teaching. Proverbs 1:8.

❖ 37 ❖

My grace is sufficient for you, for my power is made perfect in weakness.

2 Corinthians 12:9

Apostle Paul was an unequalled personality among the disciples of Jesus Christ and a man with surprisingly great revelations and visions of God. In order not to be conceited because of these exceedingly great revelations, God gave a thorn in his flesh. Paul pleaded to God on several occasions to remove this thorn from him.

Our key verse for study is the answer God gave him for this plea to remove the thorn. It is not mentioned in the Bible what this is. It can well be a bodily disease which was a discomfort to him throughout his life.

It was this grace of God that strengthened the apostle throughout his service to God and he exhorts us "Be strong, in the grace that is in Christ Jesus" (2 Timothy 2:1). We read of this 'Grace of God' at several places is the Bible.

The angel of the Lord said to Mary "greetings, you who are highly favoured! The Lord is with you" (Luke 1:28).

"The child grew and became strong in spirit" (Luke 1:80). Again, we read of Moses receiving the strength of grace from God and leading the Israelites (Exodus 33:12).

Amid trials and tribulations let us move boldly forward strengthened by the grace of our Lord.

Let us pray to our God Almighty to bestow us confidence to assert that the grace and presence of God be sufficient to lead us in times of distress.

We know for sure that "The Lord is compassionate and gracious" - Psalm 103:8

❖ 38 ❖

You cannot serve both God and money.

Matthew 6:24

The key verse here is a part of the advice given by Jesus Christ, to the crowd when he points out that it is impossible to serve God and the devil simultaneously.

In our schedule of living, we all have certain priorities. Have you ever taken time to think of this question whether our priority is to God or devil? Make doubly sure to give top priority to our Lord and Saviour. Relying on our Lord, do our duties to the best of our ability. Make sure that money alone should never be our aim in life. Money is only a commodity for use. If it is not used for the right purpose, it is purposeless. In other words, its worth depends on how we use it. For instance, a knife is a very useful item. But if it is used for killing humans, it becomes satanic and it becomes merely a tool in the hands of Satan. The same way if richness is used for the good of the community, it serves as God's purpose. Look at the Bible passage (Luke 18:24-25) where Jesus explains the difficulty of a rich man inheriting eternal life. Here our Lord points out only to the mental attitude of a rich man, i.e., to fall into Satan's way of life, the possibility is more. We can see in our midst many rich people using their riches for the good of the community, spending it in God's directed ways. A typical example is Rockefeller.

See what wise Solomon points out. Do not wear yourself out to get rich (Proverbs 23:4)

Like money, use our other riches like learning, strength etc. to serve God and his purposes. Pray to God to make us capable of that. Let us be aware of the evils of wealth. But "the wealth of the wise is their crown" - Proverbs 14:24.

❖ 39 ❖

When you pray, go into your room, close the door and pray to your father who is unseen.

Matthew 6:6

The message here is part of the teaching of Jesus Christ to the disciples and the crowd assembled at the mountain side. He started his advice with an introduction that our prayers should not be in tune with that of the hypocrites. But should be personal and private.

Prayer is in fact our plea to God. What did Bartimaeus do? He cried out to Jesus "Jesus, son of David have mercy on me" (Mark 10:47). That was his form of prayer. He got the answer and was cured of his blindness. What did Hannah do? She communicated with God, from the bottom of the heart- a silent effective prayer (1 Samuel 1:13). God heard her prayer; she was blessed with a son, Samuel. We find Jesus making a special mention of the prayer of Pharisee and the tax collector (Luke 18:10-14). The tax collector asked pardon for all the sins he committed, and he went home justified before God. What Jesus meant in our key verse is not in the literal meaning of 'the closed-door". But our minds should be free from external influences when we pray to God.

Jesus wants three things to be taken care of in our prayers.

1. Avoid publicity like the Pharisee.

2. Fix our mind wholly in God without external disturbances.

3. Put before God our requirements with cent percent belief, from the bottom of your heart.

Pray from our heart as Hannah did. God the Almighty will surely give us an answer.

Dear friend! make sure to always pray and not give up (Luke 18:1). And take the word of Theodore L. Cayler: "I do not believe that there is such a thing in the history of God's Kingdom, as a right prayer offered in a right spirit that is forever left unanswered".

❖ 40 ❖

It was not you who send me here. But God.

Genesis 45:8

The above are the words of Joseph. If we go through the life of Joseph, we find him an obedient and loving son. As per the wish of his father Jacob, Joseph went to Shechem to meet his brothers. Not finding them there, he, on his own, decided to look for them at Dothan. The love and concern shown by Joseph, for his brothers resulted in his being sold to Potiphar and from there to prison. Here, let us not forget the fact that God was with him, all through. At every step of his life, he was true to the Lord, always refraining from doing anything wrong either in word or deed, what was not right in the sight of his God. Even when he oversaw the whole land of Egypt, he never reserved any grudge or ill feeling towards these who sought after his blood.

We find Joseph, making himself known to his brothers. He "wept so loudly that the Egyptians heard him" (vs.2).

How true is the key verse, that God had sent Joseph to Egypt? Our God knows everything well ahead of us. Joseph's brothers, his beloved father, his younger brother Benjamin, all received the benefits of the good deeds of Joseph.

If we glance over this whole incident, we find that God the Almighty who was with Moses and Joshua, was also with Joseph throughout his life. To Joshua, God said "be careful to obey all the law my servant Moses gave you, do not turn from it to the right or to the left (Joshua 1:7).

Joshua followed suit and God blessed him.

Dear friends! Make sure that we do only God's will, do not turn either to your right or left. No doubt God the Almighty will be with us all throughout our life.

Remember, "The Lord will watch over your coming and going, both now and forever more" - Psalm 121:8.

❖ 41 ❖

I will not accept a thing. And even though Naaman urged him, he refused.

2 Kings 5:16

Our key verse here refers to what Elisha the man of God told Naaman when Naaman insisted to accept a gift from him. Exactly opposite was the attitude of Gehazi the servant of Elisha. After Naaman had travelled some distance, Gehazi hurried after them and under false pretext, accepted gifts, resulting in Gehazi becoming a leper.

A typical incidence of the result of greed and cheating, we read in Acts, chapter 5. Ananias and Sapphira get death penalty from Peter. Avarice and cheating are not meant for the children of God.

We find around us many who are in this habit of receiving this "misnamed present in many forms and kinds and this has now become a deadly disease in all walks of people in our society.

Dear Christian friend! Let us pray for God's grace to keep ourselves aloof from this kind of evil tendency that has become rampant in our society. Please bear in mind that "The love of money is a root of all kinds of evil" – 1 Timothy 6:10.

❖ 42 ❖

Do whatever he tells you.

John 2:5

The key verse here is the instruction of Jesus' mother to the servants who were at the wedding in Cana. Later we find Jesus instructing the servants present to fill the jars with water and to serve the guests.

In the Bible we come across many instances where Jesus is directing people to do odd jobs.

To the paralytic, Jesus said "I tell you, get up, take your mat and go home" (Mark 2:11). "To the women subjected to bleeding for 12 years, Jesus said "Go in peace" (Luke 8:48), to the man with shriveled hand Jesus said "stretch out your hand" (Mark 3:5). All these people obeyed Jesus' commands and their wish was fulfilled. Different is the case with the attendants at the wedding in Cana. They had nothing to gain by obeying Jesus' directions but obeyed without thinking of the consequences. Here also we find a miracle taking place.

Dear friend! We are in a scary world, full of hardships, and all sorts of trials and temptations. But a child of God has only one alternative, that is, to lead a life according to Jesus' commands.

Some incidents before our eyes, are indications of what we are expected to do/ not to do. Mind the checks and our conscience sometimes will be our guide.

Are we doing what our Lord Christ wants us to do? Have we ever thought of these aspects? It is time to think of this. God almighty will surely guide us.

For sure, "these commands are a lamp, this teaching is a light and the corrections of discipline, are the way to life" – Proverbs 6:23.

❖ 43 ❖

If only my master would see the prophet who is in Samaria.

2 Kings 5:3

We read in the Holy Bible, 2 Kings chap..5 the story of Naaman. Our key verse for thought are the words of a slave girl in this story to her mistress. We must note here, three aspects. First of all, the guts of a slave girl to approach her mistress on a matter (She believes to be right) especially when this subject has no relation to her assigned duties and that too at a time when slavery was rampant in that society.

Secondly, she becomes a witness to the God whom she believes. Thirdly, it is her attitude to help others. Here she was trying to help her master in whatever little way she could. The brave action of this slave girl resulted in her master getting cured. Again, we find Naaman witnessing to the world "that there is no God in all the world except in Israel" (vs.15).

At this juncture, it would be nice if we ourselves make a retrospection. In what way can we be a witness to our God, like this slave girl. Try to be in word and deed a witness to our God, at places where we had been posted by God. Surely our God expects this from His children.

❖ 44 ❖

Peter remembered the word the Lord had spoken to him. And he went outside and wept bitterly.

Luke 22:61 & 62

We find, Peter who vouchsafed that he would not at any cost disown Jesus Christ. Here we cannot counter the genuineness and sincerity when he said to Jesus "Lord, I am ready to go with you to prison and to death" (Luke 22:33). The lack of courage and mental calibre to counter the questions from the crowd, made Peter deny Christ. We should remember that Christ had already warned the disciples of such contingency, of being tempted." Pray that you will not fall into temptation" (vs.40).

Friends! Are we not also in the same situation? Peter committed a mistake, he disowned Jesus. But he repented. It is recorded that he wept bitterly, a sign of his genuine repentance. Note that he was one among the few who went early in the morning to the tomb. Again, we find Jesus appearing to him and said, "Feed my sheep" (John 21:17).

We all know the sad end of Judas, who betrayed Jesus. He did not repent as Peter did and Peter lived his whole life for Jesus and died for him.

Dear child of God! God is always ready to forgive our sins, go to him and ask for pardon. The Lord who forgave the sins of the thief at the Cross will surely forgive us, our sins. Always keep in mind that "The Lord is compassionate and gracious, slow to anger, abounding in love" – Psalm 103:8.

❖ 45 ❖

Rejoice in the Lord always.

Philippians 4:4

Our God always sought-after happiness when he created the universe. One will not be happy if he/she is alone and God created a companion for Adam. We read in the Bible, how Satan in the form of a serpent spoiled the whole setup.

In our message for thought here, Apostle Paul is exhorting the Christians in Philippi to rejoice in the Lord. To become happy, one should keep oneself free from all sorts of anxiety. A believer in Christ should be able to rejoice even during severe hardships and difficulties. Daniel kneeled and praised the Lord even while in the lion's den. Paul and Silas were praying and singing hymns to God, when thrown into prison after being severely flogged

(Acts 16:25). See what the psalmist says "This is the day; the Lord has made; let us rejoice and be glad in it (Psalm 118:24). Paul in several instances exhorts us to rejoice in the Lord. "You too should be glad and rejoice with me" (Philippians 2.18). "My brothers rejoice in the Lord" (Philippians 3:1).

A child of God should rejoice in all conditions of life, that is what Paul urges us. Money and riches and highly paid jobs are not conditions to rejoice for God's children. He should be happy in any situation in life.

Like Peter, and the psalmist, we should be able to sing, praise and rejoice in the Lord; during severe trials and extreme painful situations. Pray from the bottom of our heart to God to give us His Grace. Like David, let us sing 'praise the Lord, O my soul, all my inmost being, praise his holy name" - Psalm 103:1.

❖ 46 ❖

But when you give to the needy, do not let your left hand know what your right hand is doing.

Matthew 6:3

Our subject for thought are the guidelines Jesus gave to the crowd while addressing them to help the needy. To our mind, cash, food and clothing, normally come under the items that are being given to the needy. But I would like to include one more item. This is related to our position in the society. It is very common that many ask for help by way of recommendation / petition depending upon our official/political status in the society. Is not this also a kind of 'alms' given to the needy – the difference is, one is in cash / kind, the other is the good will of the giver. When we examine what queen, Esther did (Esther chapter 5) we find it is the most valuable 'alms' that Queen Esther gave to the Jewish community. Remember the conditions that Jesus put before the crowd. This applies here also. Years back from now, I remember quite a few people used to come to our home for help, some may not be genuine. I have heard many 'mothers' say, "any way he/she has approached us, please help" Let us not deny any one who asks for help, sometimes who knows it may make a hell of a difference to their life/career. Let us make a solemn promise that we will do our best to help the needy. Let us do it in secret as Jesus had advised the crowd. "Your father who sees what is done in secret will reward you" (vs.4) may be to you or your next generation". Cast your bread upon the waters, for after many days you will find it again (Ecclesiastes 11:1)

Dear friends! Pray that God will help us to be kind to our fellow human beings and make use of all opportunities we get to help them. Let us now decide that we "Do not say to your neighbour, 'come back later, I will give it tomorrow' – when you now have it with you" – Proverbs 3:28.

They asked him, 'What do you do? Where do you come from? What is your country? From what people are you?

Jonah 1:8

The above are a few questions put to Jonah by the sailors. Have we ever faced such questions? I mean, from our Lord God and did we ever make an occasion to be questioned this way. Only when we deviate from God's accepted way of life, we must be questioned likewise.

Here we find Jonah taking his own decision against God's direction and go to Tarshish. This was a kind of absconding from God and he was thrown out of the ship into the open sea, by the sailors. But the Lord provided a great fish to swallow him. There he cried to the Lord, his God. God gave him another chance to serve God's purpose. Here he obeyed the word of God and went to the great city of Nineveh and proclaimed to them the message of God.

Dear child of God! Have you ever disobeyed God's word and gone astray? If so, cry out to God and submit yourself to God as Jonah, did. The ever-loving Almighty God, who made Jonah do wonders for him in Nineveh will save you. Always remember that "If we confess our sins, he is faithful and just and will forgive us our sins and purify us from all unrighteousness" (1 John 1:9).

❖ 48 ❖

It is God who arms me with strength and makes my way perfect.

Psalm 18:32

The above message is part of a song which David sang at a time when he was delivered by God from his enemies including Saul. David was often surrounded by enemies and was expecting an attack any time. We find him taking courage with the words "The Lord is the stronghold of my life, of whom shall I be afraid (Psalm 27:1). Why are we anxious about any impediments that confront us? Be confident that God always strengthens and encourages us. We can say like Paul , "I can do everything through him who gives me strength" (Philippians 4:13). Does not this mean that God's presence will lead us through all trials and tribulations. In 2 Timothy 2:1, Paul exhorts "Be strong in the grace that is in Christ Jesus". This in effect means that God's grace is our strength and let us grow in his grace.

Keep in mind the Lord's assurance to Joshua. "Be strong and courageous. Do not be terrified, do not be discouraged, for the Lord your God will be with you wherever you go" (Joshua 1:9). Pray to God to lead us through the dark alleys of life's sojourn, strengthened with the power of his might and taking refuge in God, our strong fortress. Let us affirm

"In you, O Lord I have taken refuge, let me never be put to shame" - Psalm 71:1.

❖ 49 ❖

My presence will go with you, and I will give you rest.

Exodus 33:14

Our message for thought is the promise our Lord God, gave to Moses while ordering him to bring the Israel community from the land of Egypt.

This promise we find in many places in our Holy Bible. The Lord God said to Joshua "I will be with you" (Joshua 1:5); The Lord's promise to Jacob "Do not be afraid, I am with you" (Isaiah 43:5). "Go and the Lord be with you" (1 Samuel 17:37) were the encouraging words of Saul, to David, when he was going to face Goliath. Our Lord has never promised a safe sojourn, instead he promises to be with us through all the toil and drudgery, the same promise the Lord gave to our forefathers. Remember, many faithful heroes had finished their race in the strength of this promise. Let us not take it for granted what is ahead of us. We are not expected to know it.

God never reveals to his children their future and that is not God's way. But we can for sure believe in our Lord and his promises, as our forefathers did.

Let God the Almighty give us His Grace and the strength to do, honestly and faithfully, to the best of our ability what all work has entrusted us. Let us pray "Teach me, O Lord, to follow your decrees, then I will keep them to the end" – Psalm 119:33.

❖ 50 ❖

Train a child in the way he should go, and when he is old he will not turn from it.

Proverbs 22:6

All parents wish that their children should grow up as good citizens, useful to them and the community. Those who are closely associated with children should bear in mind that many factors are to be taken care of, to mould their character.

Perseverance is one aspect which the children should take care from early childhood. For this, lazy habits should be completely avoided. "Lazy hands make a man poor but diligent hands bring wealth". Here is what wise Solomon says. "Go to the ant you sluggard, consider its ways and be wise" (Proverbs 6:6). "How long will you lie there you sluggard, when will you get up from your sleep" (Proverbs 6:9).

From very early days we must discourage children from being sluggish even in little things.

Extravagance is another very important aspect where the children should be discouraged. This reminds me of the advice I received from a well-educated, and experienced, well-wisher who had served many years in foreign countries. According to him, our children should be advised to categorize our requirements into three divisions. Unnecessary, necessary and urgent. Try to avoid completely the 1st, God has provided certain amenities necessary for us. These come under the second division. The third, to be taken care when necessary. Let us try to train our children along these lines, to lead a simple way of life. Another important factor, the parents are to be careful is to avoid the availability of too much funds to children. Extra funds will likely lead them in wrong directions. Discipline is another important factor to be taken care of in our children in their routine way of life. Keeping their study room, table etc., tidy, should be part of their routine study cycle. Another important factor to be taken care of is their character moulding. As Prof B.S. Warrier has pointed out "Should we not try to prevent our children becoming criminals?". Let the parents and teachers be good examples to our children, in words and deeds. Regular family prayers in our homes where parents get an occasion, to review the day's happenings and give useful tips to the children by way of advice.

Dear friends! To our children, let us exhort, "Listen my son and be wise, and keep your heart on the right path" - Proverbs 23:19.

❖ 51 ❖

Jesus said, 'It is finished.' With that he bowed his head and gave up his spirit.

John 19:30

"It is finished" are the last words of Jesus Christ on the cross. We find, Christ, after fulfilling his duties in the world, giving up his spirit to our heavenly father.

Let us ponder for a moment (1) Are we doing the duties entrusted to us by our Lord and (2) how far is God's will covered in our attempt at it. Bear in mind that one day or other we must surrender ourselves to God.

Let us move forward each day surrendering ourselves completely to God for we are not sure when our call would come. So be ready, every moment of the day, fulfilling our duties entrusted to us by our God.

To make sure that we can surrender our spirit to God, we must follow the footsteps of Jesus Christ and shun away from actions our God hates. Christ has promised his children "I am going there to prepare a place for you and if I go and prepare a place for you, I will come back and take you" (John 14: 2, 3).

Dear friend! Paul's words in Galatians 2:20, "I have been crucified with Christ, it is no longer I who live but Christ lives in me and the life which I now live in the flesh, I live by the faith in the Son of God, who loved me and gave himself for me!", is addressed to us. Think it over.

❖ 52 ❖

Be still and know that I am God.

Psalm 46:10

When we are living in this world, always surrounded by afflictions and grievances, this message is a onetime remedy to receive God's peace and comfort by which we can hold our head high courageously.

Do not view this verse in the literal sense. Instead think quietly how our Lord Jesus Christ has led us courageously through all sorts of situations in our everyday life and firmly believe that God will be with us the rest of our lives to guide and comfort us - His children. This is what the Psalmist means by his statement in our key verse above. That is exactly what the psalmist means when he says, "God is our refuge and strength and an ever-present help in trouble" (vs.1). This Psalmist again reiterates "come and see the works of the Lord" (vs.8) "he breaks the bow and shatters the spear" (vs.9). Be strong and be of good courage for "the God Almighty is with us; the God of Jacob is our fortress" (vs.11).

Dear friend! When you wake up at night in the middle of your sleep and your subconscious mind rakes up, hundred and one thoughts, try to "know I am God" (vs.10). Surely, in the morning when you wake up, you will be an altogether different person with a carefree mind and in a very happy mood.

Let us plead to God day and night thus "May my cry come before you O Lord" – Psalm 119:169.

❖ 53 ❖

Cast all your anxiety on him because he cares for you.

1 Peter 5:7

Throughout this epistle, apostle Peter is exhorting us to lead a holy life amid trials and temptations. Anxiety or worry will be a retarding factor in our normal routine of life and our God-given natural resources will become unproductive.

In the Bible, it is often said to lay all our anxieties on the Lord. "Do not be anxious about anything, but in everything, by prayer and petition with thanks giving present your requests to God" (Philippians 4:6). By this, St. Paul did not want us to be lazy and idle but to do our duties prayerfully, to the best of our abilities, of course, putting trust always in our God, the Almighty.

Look at what our Lord Jesus Christ had told his disciples "do not worry about your life, 'what you will eat' (Luke 12:22)"; "And do not set your heart on what you will eat or drink, do not worry about it" (Luke 12:29).

God works through us only. "Diligent hands will rule, but laziness ends in slave labour" (Proverbs 12:24). "The sluggard craves and gets nothing, but the desires of the diligent are fully satisfied" (Proverbs 13:4).

Dear friend! Let us try to be diligent and do faithfully what duties God is entrusting to us. That is what Christ expects from us, his children.

Pray, "In you, O Lord, I have taken refuge; let me never be put to shame" – Psalm 71:1.

No one who puts his hand to the plow and looks back is fit for service in the kingdom of God.

Luke 9:62

Our key verse above is part of the message Jesus gave to the crowd who put excuses to follow him in his final trip to Jerusalem. It is very sad that we can even now find such people in our midst. Our Christian society has now become a group of namesake Christians and we cannot find Christians with the kind of zest found in our forefathers, when confronted with trials and tribulations. Don't we feel like running away from these, abandoning what the Lord is expecting to get from us, his children?

Personally speaking, during my life's struggle, my father used to remind me always of this key message. His advice was to approach God with our problem, seek God's direction before planning, whenever you decide, hang on and face it amongst tiny bottlenecks, here and there, with self-confidence. This way we can complete what God intended us to do. This is what I strongly believe and has been my experience in the past. A God's devotee should always be full of absolute courage.

And, "As for God, his way is perfect; the word of the Lord is flawless. He is a shield for all who take refuge in him" – Psalm 18:30.

❖ 55 ❖

And we know that in all things God works for the good of those who love him, who have been called according to his purpose.

Romans 8:28

Have we ever in the context of our daily life thought of this message written by Apostle Paul in his epistle to Romans. When we look back and ponder over the past happenings in our life, such as missing the job we very much expected and waited for, not getting a job transfer we much desired etc., have we not felt, at any time later, that all that happened were for our good.

When Abraham was directed by God, to sacrifice, his one and only son, he never understood why such a direction was given to him but he implicitly obeyed. At the last moment we find God saying to Abraham "Do not lay a hand on the boy. Do not do anything to him" (Genesis 22:12). Study the history of Moses and Joseph. They loved their God Almighty, they bestowed absolute faith in him and they were able to achieve great things for God. "By faith, Abraham, when called to go to a place he would later receive as his inheritance, obeyed and went, even though he did not know where he was going" (Heb. 11:8) with the result Abraham's family flourished and our Lord Jesus Christ is the descendent of this Abraham (Matthew 1:1-16).

Dear child of God! Believe in God, love him and work to your utmost for our Lord. Pray to God to make us say 'Yes' to all that happens to us. And take it for granted that the purposes of God about us, his children are right although we may not see.

❖ 56 ❖

Go to the ant, you sluggard, consider its ways and be wise.

Proverbs 6:6

"Proverbs" written by Solomon, son of David is a good reading material for all, even for those who do not believe in God. This book is useful for people in all walks of life, for example to select a friend to manage one's finances etc. Typical example is the key verse for our thought given here.

In our life's sojourn, we are bound to do certain things at the right time and in the right way. Our God has a specific plan for each of us. Proverbs 10:5, says "He who gathers crops in summer is a wise son but he who sleeps during harvest is a disgraceful son. This does not mean that we should be like the rich man in the parable" (Luke 12:13-21) hoarding his riches to himself.

God has entrusted us certain talents. Make use of it at the proper time and place, for the good of the humanity. That is what God expects from us, His children.

Remember "Diligent hands will rule but laziness ends in slave labour" (Proverbs 12:24).

And "The lazy man does not roast his game, but the diligent man prizes his possessions - Proverbs 12:27.

❖ 57 ❖

But Ruth clung to her.

Ruth 1:14

The book of 'Ruth' was written around 1100 B.C. Ruth was the daughter-in-law of Elimelech and Naomi, who migrated to Bethlehem in Judah. They had two sons and were married to Moabite women. Elimelech and his two sons died, and Naomi was left with her two daughters-in-law.

We find Naomi compelling her daughters-in-law, to return to their native land and their people. Ruth, even though she was a Moabite, insisted to remain with her mother-in-law and declared that "your people will be my people and your God my God" (vs.16).

It is not the volume of work or the subject we do is important in the sight of God. It is the genuineness and sincerity in our approach to what we do and all the steps that we take should be acceptable in the eyes of the Lord who is watching us all through the night and day.

Here we find Ruth standing by her mother-in-law and the God, they served. Remember, she falls in the genealogy of our Lord Jesus Christ. In the later part of the scripture we find Ruth exhibiting her lingering love to her mother-in-law. She stood by Naomi in her ups and downs.

Ruth's exemplary conduct in her approach to her mother-in-law, Naomi should be an eye opener to us in the back ground of too many marriage break ups in our present day set up. It is high time for us to think and accept that the break up in our modern family setup is the lack of this unselfish love.

Dear child of God! Right now, let us make a firm decision that we will make a sincere effort to create such an atmosphere of love and respect among the members of our family. God is present only if love is present. Heed the words of John. "There is no fear in love, but perfect love drives out fear, because fear has to do with punishment. The one who fears is not made perfect in love" – 1 John 4:18.

❖ 58 ❖

It is better to take refuge
in the Lord than to trust in man.

Psalm 118:8

We can compare our life's sojourn to a trip in a ship. Our Lord takes the place of the captain and we are passengers. However, rough the ocean may be, an experienced and well competent captain will sail the ship with care across the ocean to the port. The passengers usually never bother about what happens outside. They take it for granted that the ship's captain will take them safely to the shore. This is exactly what the Psalmist reminds us. "Commit your way to the Lord, trust in him and he will do this" (Psalm 37:5).

Here everywhere, there is an underlying truth. We do the work entrusted to us to the best of our ability, keeping God as our focal point. Each one of us is endowed with qualities of different size and content. God does not want us to sit idle like the foolish servant who dumped his coin in the earth and found fault with the giver (Matthew 25:25).

A believer wherever he is and in whatever position he is, doctor, engineer, teacher, home-maker, God does not expect him or her to take up Christian work at the cost of his or her regular duties. Where ever we are we can be a good servant of Jesus, by being an example to others by our behavior, conversation,action and how we present ourselves..

Dear friend! Make best use of the little you have (God-given talent) and God Almighty will multiply it to hundreds and thousands, for fulfilling God's purpose in this earth. Go to God and say "Here my cry O God; Listen to my prayer" – Psalm 61:1

❖ 59 ❖

For the Son of Man came to seek and to save what was lost.

Luke 19:10

Zacchaeus was asked to come down from the sycamore tree and Jesus went with him to his house. Our key verse here is part of the conversation Jesus had with him on their reaching home.

Let us realize that our Jesus is always bidding us, knocking on the doors of our heart. We alone can open it to allow Jesus to enter.

Are we willing to open our heart to God? That is what Zacchaeus did here. Jesus accompanied him to his home and he was extremely happy to have Jesus as his guest. He enjoyed peace of mind which he never had felt in his life before. History says that ever since the visit of Jesus, he became a staunch disciple of Jesus, worked for God's kingdom and lived the rest of his life in Jericho. Here one thing is certain. He realized his mistakes and repented. Besides he found his own solution. He said to the Lord "Look Lord! Here and now I give half of my possessions to the poor and if I had cheated anybody out of anything, I will pay back four times the amount" (Luke 19:8).

Dear reader! Have you committed a sin against our Lord? Correct it and repent. Take courage. Our Lord will surely enter your home and will be your guest. Remember, "Dishonest money dwindles away, but he who gathers money little by little makes it grow" – Proverbs 13:11.

❖ 60 ❖

Is anything too hard for the Lord?

Genesis 18:14

We read in the Bible that Sara laughed to herself when the angel appeared to Abraham and announced that Sara will deliver a boy. Both Abraham and Sara ignored the truth that nothing is impossible for God. Our message for thought is the question put forward by the Lord to Abraham in this context.

Yes, nothing is impossible for God. He brought the Israelites from the clutches of Pharaoh to the promised land cutting across the Red Sea. Look at what Nebuchadnezzar had certified. "No other God can save in this way" (Daniel 3:29).

We see throughout the Bible many instances emphasizing this truth. The Almighty God who raised Lazarus from the dead, who healed the demon possessed, listening to his cry, will surely listen to our cry for help when we do it with absolute faith in him.

Dear child of God! God has his 'own time and place'. Wait patiently hoping for the best. Believe, nothing is impossible to God.

Take to heart that "Those who trust in the Lord are like Mount Zion, which cannot be shaken but endures for ever - Psalm 125:1.

❖ 61 ❖

Have you entered the store houses of the snow or seen the storehouses of the hail, which I reserve for times of trouble, for days of war and battles?

Job 38:22, 23

The message for our thought are the words spoken by God to Job. We know that God's ways concerning humans are not completely revealed to us. We must accept this fact and we must read and understand the book of Job. Satan tried his level best to tempt Job. Job, a righteous man was deprived of his children, wealth and health and what not? And during all his pain and sufferings and the accusation of his friend he held on to his faith in God. He reiterated "Though he slays me yet will I hope in him" (chapter13, vs.15).

Let us have a look back at our past. Through, loss of money, loss of loved ones and other calamities, did not the God Almighty lead us safely through all these years. Trust in our Lord who can steer us through any dark alley and move forward with confidence.

What we believers must best do is to seek God's help through prayer to keep us in good stead.

Satan, in his encounter with Job finally had to admit that he had mistaken in trying to tempt Job. Job held tightly on to God's hands and sailed through safely.

The Bible says, "The Lord made him prosperous again and gave him twice as much he had before" (Job 42:10).

Let us pray that God will give us strength and courage, to go through all trials and temptations, without denying our saviour Jesus Christ.

> "God often sends me joy through pain
> Through bitter loss, divinest gain"
> Yet through it all dark days or bright
> I know my father leads aright"   Conklin

❖ 62 ❖

Thus far the Lord has helped us.

1 Samuel 7:12

These are the words of Samuel after pursuing and subduing the Philistines at Mizpah.

Try to meditate on these words everyday immediately after getting up from your bed and thank God, for the Lord our God has led us in thick and thin. Can any of God's children deny this?

Let us like apostle Paul, press on towards the goal forgetting those behind and listening to God's call, do what best you can do with what God has entrusted to you. Repent over the past sins we committed and submit ourselves before God like apostle Peter. He denied Jesus Christ, then repented and cried before God and our Lord made him the greatest of all apostles. No doubt that the same God will take you and me in his fold. "There will be more rejoicing in heaven over one sinner who repents than over ninety-nine righteous persons who do not need to repent" (Luke 15:7).

In a race, all the runners run but only one gets the prize. So, let us run to get the prize. That is what our Lord expects from us.

"But one thing I do. Forgetting what is behind and straining towards what is ahead, I press on toward the goal to win the prize for which God has called me heaven ward in Christ Jesus" - Philippians 3:13, 14. Dear child of God! Let us try to follow Paul.

❖ 63 ❖

The Lord is my Shepherd,
I shall not be in want.

Psalm 23:1

Here in the Psalm we find God and David pictured as shepherd and lamb respectively. It would be more meaningful if we try to understand this Psalm, putting ourselves in the place of David.

'I shall not be in want' in effect says that we have everything we need. If we go through the next few versus in the Psalm, we find that a good shepherd provides all that is needed for the herd, such as green grass and clear water to drink. At the same time, the shepherd is bound to look after the safety of the herds. Again, our Lord the good shepherd will make us tread through the paths of righteousness only.

Psalm 23, is simple and understandable even to children. That is why in every Christian home, parents make sure that their children invariably learn by heart, this particular Psalm before any other Bible verses. There by the children at their very early stages in life get confidence that our Lord, the good shepherd is close to them, to help face the realities of life.

See, how Jesus addressed the Pharisees after healing the blind. "I am the good shepherd. The good shepherd lays down his life for the sheep" (John 10:11).

David gained confidence and courage all through his life just because he felt and believed that Lord the good shepherd was always with him.

Dear friend! Don't be afraid in life's sojourn. Our Lord the good Shepherd will no doubt take care of you and me. He is always with us and leading us; listen to his words and follow him blindly. It is not that the Lord was, will be, will become my Shepherd. But believe strongly, the Lord will be my Shepherd today, tomorrow and always throughout my life.

"I lie down and sleep, I wake again because the Lord sustains me" (Psalm 3:5). Let us believe strongly in these words of David.

❖ 64 ❖

Why, you do not even know,
what will happen tomorrow. What is your
life? You are a mist that appears for
a little while and then vanishes.

James 4:14

James, the brother of our Lord Jesus Christ, wrote this epistle in around A.D 48 to the Christians living scattered among people of other faiths.

We find many instances in the Bible saying that our life in this earthly world is only for a short while. "They are like the new grass of the morning – "Though in the morning it springs up now, by evening it is dry and withered" (Psalm 90:5, 6). Look at the prayer of the afflicted, pointing out his lament before God. "My days are like the evening shadow, I wither away like grass" (Psalm 102:11). The words of David in Psalm 103 is noteworthy. "As for man his days are like grass, he flourishes like a flower of the field; the wind blows over it and it is gone, and its place remembers it no more" (Psalm 103:15, 16). Moses correctly points out in psalm 90, about our life here. The length of our days is short, they quickly pass, and we fly away. Listen to Paul's advice to Corinthians. "We know that if the earthly tent we live in is destroyed, we have a building from God, an eternal house in heaven, not built by human hands" (2 Corinthians 5:1).

Note the words of Jesus Christ. "In my father's house are many rooms. If it were not so I would have told you, I am going there to prepare a place for you" (John 14:2).

Friend, have we ever pondered over this abode. Have we, transit travellers, ever thought of getting there. How do we get the entry visa and how are we to get qualified for this? Jesus Christ shows the way. "Whoever has my commands and obeys them, he is the one who loves me. He who loves me will be loved by my Father and I too will love him and show myself to him" (John 14:21). "If anyone loves me he will obey my teaching, My Father will love him, and we will come to him and make our home with him" (John 14:23).

Let us love our Saviour Lord Jesus Christ and obey his commands. Use the opportunities that God has bestowed on us, for the good of humankind. Bear in our minds that we are only holders of a transit visa with a pass to go through only once. The life we have here is not all that is there. There is a far, far better place that our Lord Jesus is preparing for those who love him. Bear in mind these factors and lead a life worthy to be called the children of God.

"Every word of God is flawless; He is a shield to those who take refuge in Him" – Proverbs 30:5

❖ 65 ❖

He fell in love with a woman in the valley of Sorek whose name was Delilah.

Judges 16:4

"He", in the key verse refers to Samson, a person born of God-fearing parents after constant prayers and long waiting. He was chosen by the Lord, for the deliverance of Israel.

He was endowed with physical strength, beyond imagination, so strong that he could snap the ropes tied around his arms like charred flax (15:14). He killed a thousand humans single handed with a fresh thaw bone of a donkey.

Twenty long years, Samson was a judge over Israel. Though a chosen child of the Lord, we find him associating with women, without giving any heed to the wish of his Lord. His first marriage was against the wish of his parents, then an illegal relationship with a prostitute, and the third relationship with Delilah. We are not sure how far he loved her and how sincere his love was. But one thing was evident. Samson had a weakness for women. Delilah exploited this weakness. Forgetting the fact that he was the chosen child of the Lord he succumbs to the pressure of coaxing and nagging of Delilah, and Samson divulges the secret of his strength to her. Delilah made him sleep and got the braids of his hair removed. We read that his strength left him (vs.19) with the result, the Philistines chained him and put him in prison.

Dear young friends! watch the downfall of the chosen child of God. Be careful, that our God given blessings, brain power and muscle power, should not drive us through undesired routes to the dislike of our Lord Jesus Christ. Pray to God to keep us away from Satan's trials and gird us with strength and grace to fight and subdue such ungodly inklings. The constant presence of God in our thoughts and deeds is the best antidote to fight this.

Finally, see for ourselves, whether our love falls in the category of Samson or that of the love described in 1 Corinthians 13. Remember our God expects us to be a 'good Samaritan' and pray for the strength and courage.

You can trust God always in the dark or in the day. Make sure that you "Love the Lord, your God with all your heart and with all your soul and with all your mind" - Matthew 22:37.

❖ 66 ❖

Neither he who plants nor he who waters is anything, but only God, who makes them grow.

1 Corinthians 3:7

Apostle Paul in his epistle to the Corinthians refers to the role played by the Christian ministry and our key verse is a part of that message.

From the beginning of the creation, God has given us the freedom to choose. In other words, we are our own masters in making the choice.

In that sense, those selected by God to serve him must play their own role, of course to be backed by him.

"I planted the seed Apollos watered, and God made it grow" (vs.6). This in effect means that it is God that is playing the most important and ultimate role in the process of growth. Those who believe in God, the Almighty must bear in mind that this is the fundamental principle involved in our life's sojourn here. The door is open before us, our duty as God's children is to get his directions through prayer to decide and act accordingly. God does not expect us to stay still, keeping our hands folded expecting God to do everything for us. We must plant and water, then only God can make it grow and bear fruit. We are God's fellow makers (1 Corinthians 3:9). Only through his children can God do his part.

Jesus said to Peter, "Put out into deep water and let down the nets for a catch" (Luke 5:4). Peter obeyed and they "caught such a large number of fish that their net began to break" (vs.6).

"Christ has no hands but our hands,
To do His work today
He has no feet but our feet
To lead men in His way   Annie Johnson Flint

Dear friend! Where ever you are and what ever work has been assigned to you by our Lord, are you ready to do your best for God. Let us do what is entrusted to us with pleasure and sincerity. That is what God expects of a believer in Christ. Remember, "Lazy hands make a man poor, but diligent hands bring wealth" – Proverbs 10:4

❖ 67 ❖

The length of our days is seventy years or eighty, if we have the strength; yet their span is but trouble and sorrow.

Psalm 90:10

Problems concerning old people are being discussed very often in many platforms these days. This has now become a social issue.

This Psalm including the key verse is the prayer of David; a man of God and the Psalm mainly deals with perishable human beings. If we compare western countries, seventies and eighties never come with category of old age. In the fifties, my landlord (I was in England at that time) around eighty years of age, used to do all the odd annual maintenance of their cottage by himself.

To them being 80 or 90 years was no problem. Where do we stand? A man of 60 will be categorized as a good old man. If you are seventy or eighty, you are written off in all aspects in the society. Should not we, the children of God, endeavour to make a change in this situation. Here are the words of an old man nearing ninety.

"My health is deteriorating but my mind and will power is still strong. The feeling that God the Almighty has not forsaken me, makes me move on with courage and confidence".

It is commonly accepted that a seven-year-old and a seventy-year-old are in many ways the same. That means that they both should be treated in the same way and the love and care we normally give to a seven year old should also be given to a seventy-year-old. The youngsters should make sure that the older people in the family be treated with care and respect. That is the duty of every child of God, our God sees and knows all things and we will be rewarded in heaven.

Here is a well-known story (may be or may not be true). To a father trying to throw away a rotten plate used by his father, the son requests not to throw away the plate saying, "Father I need the plate in future". This father got the point and realizing his mistake apologized to his son – the story goes thus.

A word to the youngsters: Do what little you can do, to keep your grandparents cheerful and happy. This will always be a blessing to you.

"A wise son brings joy to his father, but a foolish son grief to his mother" (Proverbs 10:1). Is it not highly deplorable that in Kerala, where we have a large Christian population, the government must legislate rules and regulations for the welfare of the old. Senior citizens "cheer up". Hold on to psalmist's prayer "Do not cast me away when I am old, do not forsake me when my strength is gone" - Psalm 71:9.

"Honour your father and mother" – which is the first commandment with a promise – that it may go well with you and that you may enjoy long life on the earth" – (Ephesians 6:2,3). Youngsters! Bear this in mind.

Wise Solomon exhorts, "Listen, my son and be wise and keep your heart on the right path" – Proverbs 23:19.

❖ 68 ❖

The pride of your heart has deceived you, you who live in the clefts of the rocks and make your home on the heights. You who say to yourself, who can bring me down to the ground?

Obadiah 1:3

This book containing only twenty-one verses was said to be written around B.C. 587. Not much is known about him, except his name.

The '1' complex i.e., 'I am the greatest' in effect revolves round one's health, wealth and wisdom. The same factors make a country arrogant. Obadiah prophecies that the –Edomites, the traditional enemies will be punished, and the Israelites will be protected by the Lord. We find that many factors pushed the Ebonite's to be arrogant and hot-headed. Firstly, the geography of their country. They lived in the cliffs of the rocks, very tough to be attacked from outside. Secondly the people were very healthy and this muscle power to fight added to their pride.

The other day when I opened a daily; I noticed in bold letters a news "A ninety old mother was thrown into the shed by her children". My first reaction at that moment, was a simple question that came to my mind. Arrogance due to muscle power. What else?

The self-assessment of the Edomites that they possessed wisdom and prudence added to their arrogance – "In that day declares the Lord, will I not destroy the wise men of Edom, men of understanding in the mountains of Esau" (vs.8).

The prophet warns that the all-powerful God is watching and the Edomites who attacked Judah and plundered Jerusalem will be punished ultimately. "The day of the Lord is near for all nations. As you have done it will be done to you, your deeds will return upon your own head" (vs.15). All through out, the prophet gives the message that God will not go with ungodly arrogance and they will be punished.

Dear friend! Wisdom and health are the gifts of our Lord. Bearing this in mind try to be prudent, polite, God-fearing, merciful and pray God to help us to run the race that is set before us faithfully and honestly. Always bear in mind that "prides goes before destruction, a haughty spirit before a fall" – Proverbs 16:18.

❖ 69 ❖

In all these things we are more than conquerors through him who loved us.

Romans 8:37

For a believer in Christ, to conquer means, to win over temptations of Satan, like Job did, going through all kinds of temptations.

The previous verses emphatically say "who shall separate us from the love of Christ? Shall trouble or hardship or persecution or famine or nakedness or danger or sword (vs.35).

When we abandon Christ's love it ultimately ends in our being in the clutches of Satan and that leads us on to become slaves of Satan. Naturally we fall prey to all sorts of evil temptations and sin.

Apostle Paul reminds us that "neither height nor depth nor anything else on all creations will be able to separate us from the love of God that is in Christ Jesus our Lord" (vs.39).

Dear Reader! Take thought of this and that will lead us forward during our outmost difficulties. If we rewind our thoughts we can see many who when they were during hardships and persecutions, deny God and at the same time, in the centre of prosperity and abundance live a life forgetting our Master and all his teachings. This is what we find in Tolstoy's farmer, who helped others in the hard and difficult times and when he became rich he forgot his past and became arrogant and haughty. Also, we come across cases, where very faithful and god-fearing persons losing their faith in the living God and denying him during trials. Our bounden duty is to strongly believe that God punishes those whom he loves. Remember Paul's earlier days, how he stood his ground in the face of suffering (Hebrews 10:32). Look what Stephen did. Stephen full of the holy spirit looked up to heaven (Acts 7:55) and saw the glory of God. They dragged him out of the city and stoned him to death. (Acts 7:57-59). Peter rejoiced in his suffering for Christ. (1 Peter 4:13). Pray that God will help us circumvent all difficulties confronting us.

God hears us when we cry to him for mercy. Always remember that.

"No temptation has seized you except what is common to man. And God is faithful, he will not let you to be tempted beyond what you can bear" – 1 Corinthians 10:13.

❖ 70 ❖

Are you envious because I am generous?

Matthew 20:15

O ur key verse is the question put by the owner of the vineyard to the workers. When you lack in love you become envious. This is very specifically pointed out in 1 Corinthians 13. "Love is patient, love is kind, it does not envy" (vs.4) i.e. where there is love, there is no envy.

Here we find the workers joining for work in the vineyard at different times.

At the end of the day, the owner directs his work supervisor to pay their wages and the workers were paid according to the directions of the owner. When they found that the late-comers were paid the same wage as those who joined duty early in the day and who worked more hours, were slightly offended. To them, the owner asks a very natural question "Don't I have the right to do what I want with my own money" (vs.15) and adds the question given in our key thought.

At first sight this may look odd and may not look just. But when we look at God and his kingdom the question of priority, reporting 1st or last is not valid here. How well and how faithfully we did what God had entrusted to us? That is how God looks at it.

When we compare the work of one person to another, there is always an undesired effect i.e., we are not doing our best but just better than the other. That in the correct sense, is not to our maximum capacity. Our Lord expects from a believer in Christ, our maximum output, not just better than the other.

Dear friend! Do the duties entrusted to us by our Lord, to the best of our ability as per God's plan. Let the Lord address you "well done, good and faithful servant, you have been faithful with a few things, I will put you in charge of many things" (Matthew 25:23). Let us "Act with courage, and may the Lord be with those who do well" – 2 Chronicles 19:11.

❖ 71 ❖

Blessed is the man who trusts in the Lord, whose confidence is in him.

Jeremiah 17:7

When idol worship and social injustice were rampant in Judah and Jerusalem, prophet Jeremiah prophesied the inevitable punishment by the Lord and in that context his comments on those who confide and trust in him, is our key verse here.

Generally, when we want to address a person blessed, remember, there are many factors, such as wealth, health, and the like are involved in it. But when we are to address a believer as blessed, he should have some other qualifications according to prophet Jeremiah.

Blessedness is not a transient condition but is long lasting. The prophet in the later part of his message points it out clearly.

One who amasses wealth by unfair means is, to an outsider "blessed" but is like a "partridge that hatches eggs it did not lay". "When his or her life is half gone they will desert him or her and in the end, the person will prove to be a fool" (vs.11).

One who trusts in God and wholly depends on him in whatever situation he or she is in. "He will be like a tree planted by the water that sends out its roots by the stream, it does not fear when heat comes, its leaves are always green and has no worries in the year of draught and never fails to bear fruit" (vs.8). "He will dwell in parched places in the desert" (vs.6) and will be least afraid.

Remember that such a person is in the real sense blessed. According to the Psalmist, "Blessed are all those who fear the Lord, who walk in His ways, you will eat the fruit of your labour, blessings and prosperity will be yours (Psalm 128:1, 2). Again "It is better to take refuge in the Lord than to trust in man. It is better to take refuge in the Lord than to trust in princess" (118:8, 9). Also "Those who trust in the Lord are like mount Zion which cannot be shaken but endures forever" (Psalm 125:1).

Dear young friend, wait on the Lord, do what is right in His sight and live a life, giving forth useful fruits. Bear in mind that this is what our Lord Jesus Christ expects from us, his children.

> "Our strength and Hope is in the Lord
> We rest secure in His sure word.
> Although we are tempted to despair
> We know we are kept with His care"   D.De Hann

❖ 72 ❖

If the Lord delights in a man's way, he makes his steps firm.

Psalm 37:23

It can be said that this Psalm was written by David influenced by the experiences in his life. It is our age-old belief that in everything and always we are being led by our Almighty God. We are born and brought up in this back ground. It can be seen that "Begin the day with God" is the example set by Jesus Christ to us, his believers.

"Very early in the morning, while it was still dark, Jesus got up, left the house and went off to a solitary place where he prayed" (Mark 1:35).

It means that before we encounter our daily routine life we pray to God to strengthen us by his grace. Many Christian veterans and believers in Christ followed this routine. "In the morning, O Lord, you hear my voice, in the morning I lay my requests before you, and wait in expectation (Psalm 5:3) "Indeed the very hairs of your head are all numbered. Don't be afraid" (Luke 12:7). This is our Lord's promise. As such why should we be afraid and worried. Here let us bear in mind one simple advice. Do what is right in the eyes of our Lord, never deviate to the right or to the left from it. We must be able to affirm like Job. "Though he slays me, yet will I hope in him, I will surely defend my ways to his face" (Job 13:15).

Dear friend! Our Lord Jesus Christ loves every one of us. By his mercy we are led every hour and every minute of our daily life. That being the case, our Lord will give us courage and strength to encounter all contingencies in our everyday life. With the psalmist let us vouchsafe "Your Lord is a lamp to my feet and a light for my path" - Psalm 119:105.

❖ 73 ❖

I can do everything through him who gives me strength.

Philippians 4:13

During his discourse with the Philippians apostle Paul makes a reference to his personal life as noted in the key verse. He can work for Jesus Christ in any odd situation, however difficult and hard, by the grace of God who strengthens him. Only then can he say, "I am greatly encouraged; in all our troubles my joy knows no bounds" (2 Corinthians 7:4). (Bear in mind that these words were written while he was in prison). Everything implies that in any situation however hard and difficult, if one who strengthens us is with us, nothing is impossible.

Let us make a quick glance at the past Christian history, where impossible were made possible. William Carey an ordinary cobbler came to India, brought many Indians to Jesus Christ and created history. Remember, God leads us in our life's sojourn. "The gracious hand of our God is on everyone who looks to him" (Ezra 8:22). Don't forget that our forefathers went through many trials and tribulations and God wonderfully led them. Remember Paul's words "I have learned the secret of being content in any and every situation, whether well-fed or hungry, whether living in plenty or in want" (Philippians 4:12). And have we ever thought of the situation in which Paul wrote these words. Slavery was rampant then, and even while in prison through his messages he instilled courage in them and led them in words and deeds. How was he able to do it? Paul himself reveals the secret. "Christ lives in me".

Look, "Some trust in chariots and some in horses, but we trust in the name of the Lord our God" (Psalm 20:7).

But let us hold firmly to the hands of our Lord Jesus Christ and imbibing the heavenly qualities such as love, modesty, pity, and benevolence move forward with the firm hope that God the Almighty will strengthen and lead us forward. Friends! Let us "Be strong in the Lord and in His mighty power" – Ephesians 6:10.

❖ 74 ❖

Elijah went before the people and said: How long will you waver between two opinions. If the Lord is God, follow him, but if Baal is God, follow him.

1 Kings 18:21

After Solomon's reign during the rule of Ahab the Israelites slowly began to worship Baal instead of the God of Israel. There was no rain and famine were severe. We find God sending Elijah to their midst. King Ahab put the blame on the prophet for this sad state. Elijah retorted saying that "you and your father's family had abandoned the Lord's commands and followed the Baals" (vs18).

The chosen people abandoning their God had turned to worship Baal and the prophet's genuine reaction was expressed at Mt. Carmel in the words given as the key verse.

It is recorded that the crowd kept silent to this question (vs.21).

Let us make an introspection. If the question had been passed on to us, how many of us will be able to answer sincerely this question? How many of us will take a "This way or that way" stand? We believers in Christ should show the courage to differentiate between good and evil and hang on to what is right. We find a lot of examples, in the Bible of the sufferings of many for not joining hands with what they think is ungodly. "What harmony is there between Christ and Baal? What does a believer have in common with an unbeliever? What agreement is there between the temple of God and idols? For we are the temple of the living

God" (2 Corinthians 6:15, 16). Submit ourselves wholly to God and his wishes. There is no half way for a believing Christian. Let us ponder for a moment. Are we with God or with Baal? If you are in two minds, take a firm decision right now. Repent and turn wholly to God. May God bless you.

"For though a righteous man falls seven times, he rises again but the wicked are bought down by calamity" – Proverbs 24:16.

❖ 75 ❖

May your hand be ready to help me for I have chosen your precepts.

Psalm 119:173

From the very beginning of creation, God put certain conditions before humanity. They may be termed commands. The Lord God commanded the man, "you are free to eat from any tree in the garden, but you must not eat from the tree of knowledge of good and evil" (Genesis 2:16, 17).

In order to lead a life according to his wish, God, through the Bible gives us also certain other commands.

To the Israelites, the chosen nation the Lord gives commands through Moses. He should lead a life according to Lord's plans, not straying either to the left or right. The Lord also warns his people through the holy scripture the consequences of disobedience

(Deuteronomy 5:32). To Joshua, God commands" Be strong and very courageous, because you will lead these people to inherit the land I swore to their forefathers, to give them. Be strong and very courageous. Be careful to obey all the law my servant Moses gave you" (Joshua 1:6, 7). "Do not let this Book of the Law depart from your month, meditate on it day and night (Joshua 1:8).

Let us examine what Jesus before being arrested by officials of the chief priests, had told his disciples. "If you love me, you will obey what I command" (John 14:15). "If you obey my commands, you will remain in my love, just as I have obeyed my father's commands and remain in his love" (John 15:10). Obey God's word and be able to affirm like the psalmist. "Blessed is the man who fears the Lord, who finds great delight in his commands". (Psalms 112:1)

God the Almighty can provide more than what we ask for. And let us pray for his grace to seek out his commands and fulfill them.

"Every word of God is flawless; he is a shield to those who take refuge in him" - Proverbs 30:5

❖ 76 ❖

He who guards his mouth and
his tongue keeps himself from calamity.

Proverbs 21:23

We cannot but state that the tongue, a small organ in our body (This little three-ounce slab of meat) is the most dangerous. In our Bible this organ is being discussed the most. With this tongue, we praise God and at the same time use it to curse our fellow brothers. This tongue is too dangerous to jeopardize even one's own life.

Psalmist prays, "Save me, O Lord from lying lips and from deceitful tongues" (Psalms 120:2). And as such it is important to know how we can use our tongue. Look at what the Bible says. "He who guards his lips guards his life but he who speaks rashly will come to ruin" (Proverbs 13:3). "We all stumble in many ways. If anyone is never at fault in what he says, he is a perfect man, able to keep his whole body in check" (James 3:2). "No man can tame the tongue, it is a restless evil, full of deadly poison" (James 3:8).

Nothing is impossible to God and so pray God for his grace to put a muzzle on our tongue.

Jesus Christ when he appeared before the disciples after resurrection directed them "go into all the world and preach the good news to all creation" (Mark 16:15). How wonderful and blessed it is, if this, God given tongue is used "to preach the good news" to everyone in this world. James points out. "Everyone should be quick to listen, slow to speak and slow to become angry" (James 1:19). "If any one considers himself religious and yet does not keep a tight rein on his tongue, he deceives himself and his religion is worthless" (James 1:26).

A word to my young friends. The future generation is in your hands. Pray that God will provide you grace to watch your ways and keep your tongue from sin as well as to put a muzzle on your mouth in the presence of the wicked. Also, to help you to refrain from speaking lies. Our Lord who is listening to our prayers will strengthen us. Pray, "May the Lord cut of all flattering lips and every boastful tongue" - Psalm 12:3.

❖ 77 ❖

This is the day the Lord has made; let us rejoice and be glad in it.

Psalm 118:24

This Psalm 118 is considered as thanks giving song. The psalm starts and ends with summons of praise to God. The essence of this psalm is seen in the message for our thought. Let us make a request to God every day when we rise, to enable us to spend the day happily and peacefully. Our Lord takes pleasure when he finds us happy. The psalmist exhorts us to lead a joyful life without fear, taking refuge in the Lord. Know for sure it is better to take refuge in God than to trust in human. If you look around us, we can see many who run after riches and pleasures ignoring the basic principles set out by our Lord and run into ruin and ends in suicide.

Only when we make use of each day for the good of others and thereby for the glory of God, we can sincerely join hands with the Psalmist as cited in our message. Solomon's confession in Ecclesiastes (2:11) that "everything was meaningless, a chasing after the wind, nothing was gained under the sun". Real happiness, we get only through our Lord Jesus Christ (John 15:11).

Let us keep in mind the words of James "you do not even know what will happen tomorrow. What is your life? You are a mist that appears for a little while and then vanishes" (James 4:14). And with strong faith in our Almighty, let us move on and on.

Dear friend! Keep in mind Jesus's assurance "I have won the world" and during our trials and tribulations, pray God to make each day, a happy and worthy day.

So, "Come let us sing for joy to the Lord, let us shout aloud to the rock of our salvation" – Psalm 95:1.

❧ 78 ❧

Father forgive them for they do not know what they are doing.

Luke 23:34

In the gospel, according to Luke, the crucification of Jesus is very vividly and minutely described. The key message here is Jesus's first words on the cross nailed between two criminals on either side. Our Lord's concern for others even when he was suffering from excruciating pains is noteworthy. Here it should be understood that Jesus' prayer "Forgive them" was meant for the Chief Priests and the rulers.

Our Lord was upholding the principles and the moral lessons he taught us. "Good for evil" even when he was being led to be crucified. We find Jesus healing the servant of the high priest whose ear had been cut off with the sword by one of Jesus' followers (Luke 22:51).

We find Christ in his sojourn in this world (teaching us beginning with Lord's prayer) he emphasises about forgiveness. Jesus answered, "I tell you not seven times but seventy-seven times" (Matthew 18:22). When Jesus prays for forgiveness to those responsible for his crucification let us remember that our Lord is teaching us the very lesson of forgiveness. Even when he is suffering from acute pain while at the cross he accepted the plea of the thief on his side and assured him "today you will be with me in paradise" (Luke 23:43), we find that he has been forgiven of his sins.

Right now, let us make sure that we free ourselves from all sorts of sin such as anger, blasphemy, hatred etc. and be kind to love one another and to forgive one another (as God forgives our sins).

Dear friend! Take heed of Jesus' words in the parable of the unmerciful servant. "This is how my heavenly father will treat each of you unless you forgive your brother from your heart" Matthew 18:35.

❖ 79 ❖

Create in me a pure heart, O God and renew a steadfast spirit in me.

Psalm 51:10

This is the prayer of David. David committed adultery (2 Samuel 11:4). To God this is a sin of the highest order. Prophet Nathan pointed it out to David. He admitted that he had sinned against God and repented. This is the background of this Psalm.

"Create in me a pure heart" says David. Look at Jesus when he went up on a mountain side and sat down to teach them. And he said, "Blessed are the pure in heart for they will see God" (Matthew 5:8). What does this mean? How does one measure it? These are questions which come immediately to one's mind. "None has ever seen God, but God the one and only, who is at the Father's side, has made him known" (John 1:18).

A person who believes in God, does only what is right in his sight, then you can with your inner eye, see God, know God and accordingly fashion our deeds and thoughts. The heavens declare the glory of God, the skies proclaim the work of his hands (Psalm 19:1).

That way, in nature, in the birds of the sky, in the sun and the moon, we see God and continue seeing him.

When the psalmist cries out to create a pure heart in him, it involves many truths. Let us see what they are. David prays to take away from him evil thoughts, such as selfishness, jealousy, craze for riches, and instill in him Godly thoughts such as love, kindness, humility and patience. Also, he seeks sincerely an honest, just and true heart apart from a strong Godly power and make him an entirely new creature in all spheres of life.

"Wash away all my iniquities and cleanse me from my sin. Again "wash me that I will be whiter than snow", thus goes the prayer of David.

When you have a pure heart and a steadfast spirit, Satan will have no place in our thinking.

Dear reader! Let us make an introspection. Where do we stand in the eyes of the Lord? Are we close to his heart? Do we have a place in Jesus' heart?

> "Love is an attitude, love is a prayer
> For someone in sorrow, a heart in despair".
> Anonymous.

Remember St. Paul's words:

"Whosoever sows sparingly will also reap sparingly and whosoever sows generously will also reap generously" - 2 Corinthians 9:6.

❖ 80 ❖

Your heavenly Father knows that you need them.

Matthew 6:32

To a believer, the Holy Bible is his guide. The beginning of Lord's prayer with the words. "Our father in heaven" means that we believe that God is our father.

Jesus Christ emphasises this fact when he says, "Look at the birds of the air, your heavenly father feeds them" (vs.26). "How God clothes the grass of the field which is here today and tomorrow is thrown into the fire, will he not much more clothe you" (vs.30). To our Lord, everything he has created is important. Each one of us millions and millions in this world, are different from the other (even the finger prints differ from person to person), it is then foolish to think that God who knows our slightest movements will turn a deaf ear to our needs. Ask it will be given to you, 'seek and you will find' are the words of advice of Christ to the people. If that is the case, it is the duty of every believer to know for sure that God will fulfill our needs.

In this context, a story comes to my mind and is narrated below. A father goes with his son to a faraway school to leave him at the hostel for his studies. As usual with every Christian home, the boy's mother reminds him that he should read the Bible (kept along with the clothes) daily, to which the son said 'yes'. When the father put him in the hostel and was saying goodbye, his son with tears in his eyes , told his father that he had forgotten to take his sports shoes. The father then replied "Don't worry son,

I know that you will need it and I have kept it already with your luggage."Tears of joy fell from his eyes.

Dear friend, bear in mind that our God who knows best, keeps in store for us, what all we need and is best for us. And from our part do the best we can and leave the rest to God. Take it for sure, "though you are evil, know how to give good gifts to your children, how much more will your father in heaven give good gifts to those who ask him" (Matthew 7:11).

Dear friend! Always keep in mind that "surely the arm of the Lord is not too short to save, nor his ear too dull to hear" – Isaiah 59:1.

❖ 81 ❖

Search me, O God, and know my heart, test me and know my anxious thoughts.

Psalm 139:23

In this Psalm, David describes at length a God that is omnipresent, omnipotent and all knowing. This Psalm can be a onetime remedy (panacea) for our trials and tribulations in life. It inspires us to be cheerful during our failings and strengthens us to face the various challenges that we come across in life's journey, with courage and will power. This inspirational and confidence building Psalm can be singled out as the king among all the Psalms.

"You know when I sit and when I rise, you perceive my thoughts from afar" (vs.2). How comforting it is to know that God is with us and guides us in all our affairs, all through our life, from birth to death. There is nothing about us that is hidden from God. And like a shadow, He follows us everywhere, in whatever situations we are. That is what gives us strength and courage in life's journey. God is one who knows everything and without him we get nowhere. David's plea which he makes in today's key verse given above comes from the bottom of his heart; he wants himself to be tested about his anxious thoughts and opens to God to see if there is any offensive way in him so that he can travel the path leading to everlasting life (vs.24). If we refuse ourselves to be tested, if we run away from facing life and wander aimlessly it will only lead us to our self-destruction. Because such an attitude is the result of our finding no peace of mind despite having all material comforts and luxury.

So, let us face the facts. There is no running away from God's presence. Because as David says, "If I go up to the heavens, you are there, If I make my bed in the depths, you are there" (vs.8). So, let us pray to God along with David "to have mercy on us, to blot out our transgression according to his great compassion, to wash all our iniquity and cleanse us from our sins" (Psalm 51:1-2) and at the same time plead with him to hear our prayer and let our cry for help come to him - Psalm 102:1.

❖ 82 ❖

We all stumble in many ways.

James 3:2

What apostle James points out here is a universal truth in as much as there is no one who has not stumbled and fallen into sin. This could happen in words as well as deeds. We can all see and hear that the sins committed by tongue are a daily occurring. When such failings in life happen, we are conscious of the fact that these are prompted by temptation. In the Lord's prayer, Jesus teaches us that we should be on our guard not to be led into temptations.

In the key verse given above apostle James underlines the fact that all of us repeat sinners, ever since Adam and Eve committed the first sin of disobedience to God. We have, therefore to find out ways and means to keep ourselves away from these pitfalls. The one and only remedy for this is undoubtedly PRAYER. Remember what Christ told his disciples "pray that you will not fall into temptations" (Luke 22:40). Prayer is not a once or twice a day affair. It is to be carried out constantly and consciously. Peter sinned but repented and prayed and the Lord forgave him. And he was called upon to do God's work even in the face of death – a rock on which the Church was to be built. When we are tempted and commit sins, repent and open ourselves before God through prayer, by confessing our failings. And the all forgiving God will restore us according to his mercy. Like David, let us submit ourselves to God and beseech him "to blot our transgressions, wash away all our iniquity and cleanse us from our sins" (Psalm 51:1-2). And then we can be assured that "he has removed our transgressions from us as far as the east from the west" (Psalm 103:12).

God's forgiveness is absolute and unconditional. He neither keeps a count or remembers our sins, once we have repented and confessed them. We, who by nature are weaklings, may stumble again and again and fall. But the forgiving God will put forth his hand and bring us back on our feet. We only must trust in him and submit ourselves totally to his will. In certain moments of weakness, we may relapse into sin. But go back to the Lord and fall at his feet and seek his forgiveness and he will cleanse us from our sins. Thereafter God will restore to us the Joy of his salvation and grant us a willing spirit to sustain us all through our life – Psalm 51:12.

❖ 83 ❖

I am the Lord's servant,
may it be to be as I have said.

Luke 1:38

These are the words of Mary when the angel of the Lord, Gabriel was sent to Nazareth to tell her that "you are highly favoured. The Lord is with you ... "Mary, you have found favour with God and will be with the child and give birth to a son, Jesus... for nothing is impossible with God". The description of the birth of Jesus is found only in the gospels of Matthew and Luke.

For the birth of Jesus, God chose Mary and for that of John, Elizabeth. God chooses only humans to execute his plans. Therefore, every believer must submit himself/herself to God so that we can be used by God as he has willed for each one of us. If Abraham is known as the father of all believers, Mary can be appropriately named as the mother of all who trust in God. That is why Elizabeth when filled with the Holy Spirit exclaimed to Mary, "Blessed are you among women" (Luke 1:42).

To fulfill God's plan, he needed a Mary whom he chose her, though she was betrothed to Joseph. Mary did not think twice about the social consequences of an unmarried women getting pregnant or the possible reactions of a man to whom she was already engaged, and she stands firmly determined to abide by the words of the angel. When Mary proclaimed, "I am the Lord's servant" (vs.38) it carried with it a commitment, meaning there by that she is prepared to surrender herself completely to God's will. What is it that gave Mary the inner strength to face any consequences and hostile situation? It came from the words of the angel "you who are highly favoured ... the Lord is with you" and thereby she gathered the strength to place her trust completely in God and utter the key verse given above. All of us who are believers should similarly attain such strength to face life's realities and surrender ourselves unconditionally to God who in turn knows what is good for us.

Let me recall an anecdote involving an English priest who while out for a morning walk, in the depressing English winter season, came across a man working in his field. He addresses him and says, "Good morning friend". The man out of sorts with himself and working in an inclement weather retorts curtly that he sees nothing good about the day. When the priest returns after his walk, he comes across the same person, all happy and smiling and stops to know the reason for this sudden change in his attitude. The man replies that it was indeed a good morning for him since he had the good news of being blessed with a grandchild. This goes to teach us that if we give up ourselves completely to God, there is neither good or bad in any of our days, because nothing can happen to any of us without God. "Even the very hairs of your head are numbered - fear you not therefore" (Luke 12:7). So, let us submit and surrender ourselves completely and without any reservation to God's will and then we will realise that all our days are good according to God's plan.

❖ 84 ❖

And he brought him to Jesus.

John 1:42

What is brought out in the above verse is the circumstance in which Jesus first met his disciples. When John the Baptist, with his two disciples saw Jesus passing, he exclaimed. "Look the lamb of God. Hearing this, both the disciples of John followed Jesus. One of them was Andrew, Simon Peter's brother". And we read that "the first thing Andrew did was to find his brother Simon (vs.41) and perhaps Andrew was the first one to witness for Christ when he declared. "We have found the Messiah". We may see this as an ordinary event. Look at our own commune when a person goes abroad and lands in a job, thereafter he tries to take his near and dear ones across as well.

This is also what happened during the early years of the Church. This reminds us, that service to God, ought to begin from each of our homes. Andrew shares the good news of witnessing for Christ first with his brother. We also read in the book of Kings about the captive Israelite girl, whom the commander of the king of Aram, Naaman employed as a maid in his home. This very same ordinary slave girl turned out to be a powerful witness to the Lord when she persuaded Naaman's wife to request Naaman to go to prophet Elisha to get himself cured of his leprosy. After his initial resistance, when Naaman was ultimately cured of his leprosy, the all-powerful commander of the Aramean Army himself became a witness to God, when he declared "Now I know that there is no God in all the world except in Israel" (2 Kings 5:15).

In Christ's journey on earth, to cleanse human of his original sin, there were ten more disciples apart from Andrew and Simon. There were even women who came forward to spread Christ's kingdom on earth and who supported the cause out of their own means (Luke 8: 2, 3). Many a time we came across accusations that those who are engaged in spreading the word of Christ, neglect their own homes resulting in a negative image. While it is necessary to organize various spiritual programmes such as Bible classes, prayer groups, community meets etc., by well-meaning Christian workers, they will do well to remind themselves that God does not expect them to carry out his work at the expense of neglecting their primary responsibilities such as bringing up their own children in God's ways or taking care of aged parents. God has chosen each one of us to carry out his work as effectively as we are capable of, from the worldly positions or work places where we have been placed by him. Therefore, let us pray to God to give us the grace to lead a true Christian life as expected of us from Him.

❖ 85 ❖

If God is for us who can be against us?

Romans 8:31

This key verse from Paul's epistle to the Romans is a reiteration of his unswerving faith in God that Paul had acquired through his own experience in life. This verse is often quoted as one with the most in-depth meaning in the entire Bible.

In the hustle and bustle of day-to-day life, a believer must remember to trust in the protective cover given to him by Christ Jesus. The Psalmist underlines this when he writes "For he will command his angels concerning you to guard you in all your ways, they will lift you up in their hands, so that you will not strike your foot against a stone" (Psalm 91:11, 12). Apostle Paul also gives the same message in his epistle to the Philippians. "I can do everything through him who gives me strength" (ch. 4, vs:13). In our earthly journey we will face privations, miseries and personal setbacks and the loss of our near and dear ones in our lives. These are testing times when we must anchor our faith in God. And to help us to cement this faith in God we must constantly reach for the word of God and gather courage and strength from there to overcome them. "Who shall separate us from the love of Christ? Shall trouble or hardship or persecution or famine or nakedness or danger of sword?" These words in Romans 8:35 gave the assurance, hope and strength to our forefathers to carry forward God's work in the face of heavy odds. History records that Luke was hung from a tree in Greece, Mark was dragged through the streets till he was dead, and Jacob was beheaded in Jerusalem. They were all brave and strong soldiers of Christ who willingly accepted martyrdom for Christ. All of them faced death reiterating their commitment that neither hardship, trouble, persecution, famine or even the threat of their lives could separate them from the love of Christ.

Dear friends in Christ! Let us reassure ourselves each day trusting in the everlasting love of God. Each of us should proclaim our trust and faith in God in the manner shown by Apostle Paul, that nothing can separate us from God's love and move forward seeking the Grace of God to help us fulfill the responsibilities and duties given to each one us by the Lord. Then we will be able to sing along with the Psalmist. "Those who trust in the Lord are like Mount Zion, which cannot be shaken but endures for ever-" Psalm 125:1.

❖ 86 ❖

If we have food and clothing, we will be content with that.

1 Timothy 6:8

In apostle Paul's journeys carrying the witness for Christ across lands, Timothy was a devoted helper. In this epistle to Timothy, Paul cautions him to be wary of false teachers and to resist teachings they try to spread against the one he has all along been teaching as the true message of Christ. Historians record that this epistle was sent by Paul from Macedonia around AD 65.

Those whose teachings are not compatible with the word of God that Christ taught, are not only ignorant of the real meaning of the Christian message but are also perverse in their intention. They spread such unfounded teachings with their own selfish motives for material benefits and with a view to dividing the believers. This is exactly what Paul tries to bring out. Today's key verse also underlines the futility of a life that is aimed only at amassing wealth and material possessions. The verse preceding this points out to the emptiness of such a life. "For we brought nothing into the world, and we can take nothing out of it". Let us read these verses along with what Solomon says, which is the same message given by Paul. "Give me neither poverty nor riches but give me only my daily bread" (Proverbs 30:8) and "people who want to get rich fall into temptation and a trap and into many foolish and harmful desires, that plunge into ruin and destruction" (1 Timothy 6:9). Is this not a modern phenomenon that come across each day?

Is it not a sad and dangerous trend when we see the new generation running after material luxuries and status symbols, without ever giving any thought to its adverse consequences. It is nothing but the arrogance of wealth when one comes across a fleet of luxury cars in front of the palace-like villas exhibiting sheer vulgarity of money and all the attendant "Show off"" of wealth, some of them that could be ill gotten. None of these people realize, that at the end of the day, an inevitable law of "Divine Justice, will overtake them, turning the rich of today into the pauper of tomorrow". Solomon, therefore goes one step further and calls upon us, "If your enemy is hungry, give him food to eat, if he is thirsty, give him water to drink" - Proverbs 25:21.

❖ 87 ❖

He saved others, but he cannot save himself.

Matthew 27:42

These were the words of the chief priest, the teachers of law and the Church elders after Jesus was nailed to the cross. Here also Satan is at work taunting and tempting Jesus through the chief priests and the law makers. It is the same evil force that tempted Jesus in the desert when he was hungry after fasting for forty days, by capitalizing on his physical state of hunger taunting him to turn stone into bread. Satan is always around us like a roaring lion seeking whom to devour. Not only the chief priests and the elders, but even those who passed by hurled insults on Jesus, shaking their heads which Satan thought would provoke Jesus further. Satan turns up in many forms and shapes to get the children of God off the path of righteousness. And he started his diabolic plan by taking the form of a snake in the garden of Eden.

Suffering and humiliation on the Cross was the greatest challenge that Christ faced during his life on earth, and at the very end of his life. All the same, he knew much before he was chosen by the father to come down to earth to redeem us sinners that he will have to go through this test of fire. We read about this impending test by fire and to culmination on the cross at Calvary given at different stages in the Bible. He fore told this to the crowd that followed him everywhere who failed to realize its implication. "No one takes it from me, but I lay it down on my own accord. I have authority to lay it down and authority to take it up again. This command I received from my father" (John 10:16). Isaiah prophesied this self-surrender long ago. "He was oppressed and afflicted, yet he did not open his mouth; he was led like a lamb to the slaughter and as a sheep before her shearers is silent; So, he did not open his mouth" (Isaiah 53:7).

In Gethsemane, the words uttered by Jesus when one of his companions drew the sword and cut off the ear of the servant of the high priest, are proof enough that he had already overcome and came out victorious conquering death. The sarcastic and insulting comments by the high priests and elders asking Jesus to come down from the cross were the last and worst challenge thrown at Christ and on the Cross itself. There is a truth and a mystery that is hidden here which might have surprised the high priests, the thieves on the Cross and passers-by, but which they could never comprehend. How could the one who performed miracles – turned water into wine at Canna, fed a crowd of five thousand with five loaves and even resurrected Lazar from the dead gave himself up so easily on the cross. Apostle Paul gives the answer in Colossians 1:26 "The mystery that has been kept hidden for ages and generations but is now disclosed to the saints". Jesus had the final word against the mocking high priests and law makers – "Father into thy hands I commend my spirit" (Luke 23:46).

My friends in Christ! Jesus came into this world to take our sins upon himself the burden of all our sins. Let us realize this eternal truth and try to live a life befitting this great sacrifice. "My children, I will be with you only a little longer… where I am going, you cannot come…. Love one another as I have loved you" (John 13:33, 34).

❖ 88 ❖

He will never leave you, nor forsake you, Do not be afraid, do not be discouraged.

Deuteronomy 31:8

All along the Holy Bible we come across a promise and assurance that carries an eternal truth. Here Moses gathers all the Israelites and conveys to them the words the Lord has spoken to him. "The Lord will walk before you and he will go with you and be with you". That is the promise that strengthens us and makes as courageous. The Bible teaches us that for a believer the word "FEAR" should not be in his dictionary and it has no place in his life. In the above key verse itself, along with the assurance for courage and fearlessness, the reasons for the same is also given.

Let us look at the ways the Lord repeatedly gives us the assurance. "You, O Israel, my servant Jacob whom I have chosen…. I have chosen you and have not neglected you; so, do not fear, for I am with you" (Isaiah 41:10). So, when the Lord is with us there is no place for fear in our life. Throughout the days of Christ's ministry on earth, he kept on instilling a sense of fearlessness into his disciples. "Don't be afraid, you are worth more than many sparrows" (Luke 12:7) sold for two pence

Let us look at another side of fear. We always consider that a life lived in the fear of God is a sign of obedience and service to God. "Blessed are all who fear the Lord, who walk in his ways (Psalm 128:1). In other words, our fear of God should be based on dependency on God and the love of God – a respectful love. This enables us to lead a life with God always on our side. Jesus asked his disciples, "Why are you so afraid. Do you still have no faith" (Mark 4:40)? Such fear comes from a lack of faith in God. Remember what Jesus said to Jairus, the synagogue ruler when told that his daughter was dead. The man who came from the house of Jairus thought it was futile to bother Jesus once the child was dead. Jesus ignored them and told the synagogue ruler, "Don't be afraid, just believe" (Mark 5:36).

The great gospel preacher John Chrysostom was noted for his fight against all kinds of fear. Those in power banished him from the country. Then he asked himself "why should I fear and about what? I am not afraid of death because I live in Christ." He recalled what apostle Paul had to say, "For me to live is Christ and to die is gain" (Philippians 1:21). So, Chrysostom never feared his banishment and with his unfailing faith in God, he turned out to be crusader for Christ. Let us therefore remind ourselves about the blessing that Moses pronounced on the Israelites before his death. "The eternal God is your refuge and underneath are the everlasting arms (Deuteronomy 33:27) and surrender ourselves unconditionally to God. Then we will be able to sing along with the psalmist "Even though I walk through the valley of the shadow of death, I will fear no evil, for you are with me, your rod and your staff, they comfort me" (Psalm 23:4).

❖ 89 ❖

Go into all the world and preach the good news to all creation.

Mark 16:15

These are the words that Jesus spoke after rising from the dead on the third day. Jesus appeared to the eleven disciples as they were eating. Jesus called Peter by name and commanded him "Feed my lambs". What was the advice the risen Christ gave his disciples? "All authority in heaven and on earth has been given to me. Therefore, go and make disciples of nations, baptizing them in the name of the Father, and of the Son and the Holy Spirit and teaching them to obey everything I command you" (Matthew 28:19, 20).

Here, what is noteworthy, is the delegation of the divine authority by Jesus to his disciples. In other words, neither the disciples nor any one of us, is anything, unless the spirit of God is with us.

Jesus appears to the disciples when they were totally disenchanted and downcast; despite they being witness to crucifixion and resurrection of Christ? When do we become witness to Christ? When we tell others with conviction whatever we have heard and seen about him and received from him as spiritual gifts. Hear the witness of Peter, the rock on which Christ built his church. "We did not follow cleverly invented stories when we told you about the power and coming of our Lord Jesus Christ, but we were eyewitness of his majesty (2 Peter 1:16). What the Lord desires of us is to share our experience of him with others, to be his witness to our near and dear ones, and all around us. After getting rid of the evil spirit out of the man who was possessed, what Jesus required of him was "go home to your family and tell them how much the Lord has done for you and how he has had mercy on you" (Mark 5:19).

This is what we can do for Christ, in return for the greatest sacrifice in history when he carried our sins on the cross even unto death. We are called upon to share with others what the Lord has done to us and the path he has shown us and the lessons he has taught us. Even during his ministry on earth, he sent out his twelve disciples to go 'to the lost sheep' of Israel and preach the message that the kingdom of God is near (Matthew 10:7). And the risen Christ commanded them "to go and make disciples of all nations" (Matthew 28:19).

The responsibility and mission of the church today is to go out and preach to those peoples and nations who are ignorant of the message of Christ. Any missionary work should be an effort to put into practice, what the Lord has taught us in his prayer. "Your kingdom come, your will be done on earth as it is in heaven".

Dear friends in Christ! Wherever we have been placed, whatever is the work we have been assigned by God, try to lead the life of a true Christian and there is no better missionary work.

But let us introspect and ask ourselves an honest question. Do those who watch us at our work place, at our home, in the neighbourhood, in the community, even in our social and political inter action, see Christ in us? Do we who call ourselves Christians, have the true spirit of Christ in us, in our thought, words and deeds? How many of us can come out with an honest positive answer?

❖ 90 ❖

Blessed are the merciful,
for or they will be shown mercy.

Matthew 5:7

This is part of a comprehensive set of teachings that Jesus imparted to his disciples when they came to him, after Jesus went upon a mountain and sat down, away from the crowd. Here Christ describes the qualities that are required to be a person after God and of God. A believer must practice these as a whole and not in parts. Let us therefore examine today's key verse. Love and mercy are the two sides of the same coin. Where there is mercy there is the presence of God always. Mother Teresa went into the streets of Kolkata out of mercy towards the deprived, lost and marginalised and shared her love and mercy with the unwanted and downtrodden. Listen to David's prayer seeking God's mercy. "Have mercy on me, O God according to your unfailing love, according to your great compassion, blot out my transgressions. Wash away all my iniquity and cleanse me from my sin" (Psalm 51; 1, 2). Mercy is a gift of God. God tells Moses "I will have mercy on whom I have mercy and I will have compassion on whom I have compassion" (Romans 9:15). Both the Pharisee and the tax collector went up to the temple to pray; and who went home justified before God? Not the pharisee who prayed about himself but the tax collector who stood at a distance and prayed. "God have mercy on me a sinner" (Luke 18:13). We must plead before God for his mercy from the bottom of our heart; then only we will be justified in the eyes of God like the tax collector.

Jesus advises the expert in law, who approached him for showing him the way to inherit eternal life – "to love your neighbour as yourself" and to go and show mercy to anyone needing help in distress, like the good Samaritan.

We will do well to recall an air accident involving a U.S. plane in 2009, when due to engine failure it was forced to crash land and when the captain announcing the impending disaster, all the 155 on board held their breath praying for their lives. The captain successfully force landed the plane on river Hudson, without harm or loss of life to anyone on board. The passengers were all praise for the captain and the crew and came forward to thank them, profusely for saving their lives. But just one person looked up toward heaven and praised God for giving all of them a second life. This incident reminds us of the ten lepers whom Jesus healed on his way to Jerusalem "Only one of them when he saw that he was healed, went back praising God in a loud voice". He threw himself at Jesus feet" (Luke 17:15, 16). It is significant that Luke underlines the fact that this man was a Samaritan – a foreigner. And Christ himself points out "were not all ten cleansed? Where are the other nine? Was no one found to return and give praise to God except this foreigner" (vs.17-18).

My friends in Christ! Let us introspect and ask ourselves, whether we have been lacking in gratitude to God and indifferent towards him for all the blessings and mercies he has showered upon us all these years, even though we sinners deserve nothing on our own except through his grace. All the same, "the Lord is compassionate and gracious, slow to anger, abounding in love" (Psalm 103:8). Great is his faithfulness; How about our faithfulness towards him?

Do not let your hearts be troubled.
Trust in God, trust also in me.

John 14:1

The pass over supper was over and still assembled in the room, the disciples were very much disturbed. Fear and sorrow filled their hearts. They had an inner feeling that something was wrong. They felt that they were alone in a totally unfriendly world. It is here that Jesus words given as our key verse has much significance. The advice here gives a feeling that Jesus had, in mind that he was going to be crucified.

We do not notice much concrete description about Jesus' life after death during his conversation with the disciples. But we find that he clearly states one thing i.e., "In my father's house are many rooms.... I am going to prepare a place for you" (John 14:2).

After the act of washing disciples' feet, we find Jesus giving a set of commands before leaving them. "I will be with you only a little longer" (John 13:33). As I have loved you, you must love one another" (John 13:34).

"Do not let your hearts be troubled" implies that one should keep cool. The antidote is also given in the next passage i.e., "trust in God and trust also in me".

In the Holy Bible, we can find guidelines to secure peace of mind "Take courage, it is I" said Jesus when they cried out of fear, seeing him walking on the waves (Matthew 14:27). In David's words, "Though an army besiege me, my heart will not fear, though a war break out against me, even then will I be confident" (Psalm 27:3). "Whoever lives in love, lives in God" (1 John 4:16).

"There is no fear in love, but perfect love drives out fear because fear has to do with punishment. The one who fears is not made perfect in love" (1 John 4:18). In effect, when our heart is filled with God's love, we get everlasting peace of mind.

Friend, our God knoweth all things. Nothing is hidden from him. "The eyes of the Lord are everywhere keeping watch on the wicked and the good" (Proverbs 15.3). "Are not two sparrows sold for a penny? Yet not one of them will fall on the ground apart from the will of your father". (Matthew 10:23).

Therefore, let us bear in mind the advice our Lord has given to his disciples and do the duties entrusted to us. Let us make a firm decision that we will live for our Lord each day granted free to us. May the Lord Almighty help us to accomplish this task. And "Trust in the Lord forever, for the Lord, the Lord is the rock eternal" – Isaiah 26:4.

❖ 92 ❖

Jesus said to the woman, "your faith has saved you, go in peace."

Luke 7:50

These are the words spoken by Jesus to a woman branded as a sinner.

Let us analyse the situation a little more deeply. This woman (Mary Magdalene) who had a sinful life learned that Jesus was eating at the Pharisee's house. She had heard of Jesus and his healing powers.

It might be that she was aware of the incident where Jesus healed the paralytic to make Pharisee's know that "the Son of Man has authority over earth to forgive sins" (Luke 5:24). That was why she had come to the Pharisee's house and was determined to meet Jesus Christ to get her sins forgiven. During those times it was customary to provide water to the guests to wash their feet. Knowing that such customary duties were not fulfilled, this woman brought an alabaster jar of perfume, stood crying at Jesus' feet and began to wet his feet with her tears. She wiped them with her hair, kissed them and poured perfume on them" (Luke 7:38). And Jesus said to the woman, "your sins are forgiven" (vs.48). Go in peace. Filled with unspeakable joy, on her sins being completely forgiven, we find herself dedicating fully to Jesus Christ, her Saviour. It was this extreme joy of getting her sins fully forgiven that made her follow Jesus Christ till his death. Again we see that she was the last to leave the cross after his crucifixion and the first to get to the tomb very early. It was this very sincere love that made her wait at the tomb even after all others had left (John 20:10). We find that Jesus first appeared to Mary after resurrection (Mark 16:9).

Let us here examine a question Jesus asked to Simon. "Which of them will love him more?" (Luke 7:42) and the answer Peter gave. "I suppose the one who had the biggest debt cancelled". Mary Magdalene comes under the category of one whose, full debt has been written off and hence this love and the reaction was seen throughout her life after meeting Jesus. A true story (which I happened to read) of the wonderful effect of getting our sins forgiven is briefly narrated below.

William Mackey was the son of a very devout Christian mother and both led an ideal Christian life. When he left home for higher studies it so happened that he got into a group of nonbelievers leading a life very different life from that he and his mother led. One day William, taking wine in a glass and mocking the Lord's last supper, shouted. "This is the blood of Christ". Alas! He started shivering from top to bottom, the glass fell from his hand. He ran out of the room. His conscience pricked him, he wandered in the streets like a mad man and managing to reach his room, he closed himself up in his room crying to God. His loving mother heard his cry and she ran to him and embraced him. Both prayed to God for forgiveness. From that moment onwards, he accepted Jesus Christ as his Saviour.

Mr. William Mackey lived the rest of his life as a priest and is best remembered for his gospel hymns.

Dear friends! If it so happened that we tend to become slaves to sin, repent and seek pardon, God, our heavenly father will surely forgive and take us into his fold. Remember this verse "For I will forgive their wickedness and will remember their sins no more" – Hebrews 8:12.

❖ 93 ❖

Jesus looked at him and loved him.

Mark 10:21

A large crowd including children followed Jesus during his journey across Jordan. He healed the sick and taking children in his arms, he blessed them. It was then a young man, who came running to him and fell on his knees and he confronted him with a question, "What must I do to inherit eternal life". It was there "Jesus looked at him and loved him" as in our key verse.

Many aspects involved here came to my mind.

At the first look itself, Jesus loved him. Also, he understood him, and he knew that something was lacking in him. But he still loved this young man.

We must bear in mind that our Jesus loves us also, not because we are perfect, but knows us from within . Our Lord knowing full well this young man and his drawbacks suggested to him to rectify his faults. His wealth stood in his way of following Jesus and we see here the young man, whom Jesus loved, had to retreat, sad and disappointed.

Let us understand that our wealth as such is not a sin in its own. Only when wealth stands in the way of following Jesus, this so-called wealth acts as a Satan. We find many instances in our Bible where people like Abraham and Job, though very rich, they never sacrificed their Godly principles to acquire wealth. In other words, they cared more for God and God given morals, than in worldly wealth.

In our text the young man loved wealth more than God and had to go back disappointed after meeting our Lord Jesus. We find him coming to God in right earnest to inherit eternal life. "No man can both sup and blow at once".

That is why we see him retrace his steps in despair.

Dear young friend! Our Lord Jesus Christ loves you and me. He is asking us the same question he asked to the bright young man. Whom do you prefer? God and his love or Satan? Let us examine ourselves with an open mind.

In the words of Jesus Christ, "It is easier for a camel to go through the eye of a needle than for a rich man to enter the kingdom of God" – Mark 10:25.

❖ 94 ❖

My son keep your father's commands and do not forsake your mother's teaching.

Proverbs 6:20

The most blessed aspect of one's life is to have a mother who leads a dedicated prayer life. Mother, father, teacher, God is the accepted code that we have been hearing all along.

In today's increasing extravagant life style, the question of how much respect is given by the children to their parents is a matter of much discussion. Parents get a 'don't care' attitude from their children after they grow up and can stand on their feet. This, as we can see in our everyday normal life, brings a lot of heartache to our aged parents. Generally, it is said that the daughter-in-law is the main 'culprit'. The son talking freely to his mother in the absence of his wife, shunts away when his wife appears in the scene, is a common sight in many families.

The grown-up children should bear in mind that their parents leaving aside all their needs and desires, amidst physical, financial,relational problems bring up their children with high hopes. Let the young parents think for a moment whether they are giving legitimate care and respect to their old parents.

In many Christian families, an advice to their daughters, is that they are to be sent in marriage to another house and the parents in the new home are her new parents and to look after them is part of her duties. One must bear in mind that treating your parents with respect, love and care is more acceptable to our Lord than conducting or participating in group prayer meetings, reading the Bible etc., like Pharisees. This statement should not be misinterpreted that one should not have such prayer meetings and the like.

Dear young friends! It would be wise that you sit and ponder over, that your pride owing to your present good health has always a duration and a limit.

Here is the approach of a father to his son, as envisaged by our Lord Jesus Christ. "Which of you fathers, if your son asks for a fish, will give him a snake instead? Or if he asks for an egg will give him a scorpion"? (Luke 11:11, 12). Please always bear in mind "A wise son brings joy to his father; but a foolish man despises his mother" - Proverbs 15:20.

❖ 95 ❖

No discipline seems pleasant at the time,
but painful. Later, however it produces
a harvest of righteousness and peace
for those who have been trained by it.

Hebrews 12:11

Have you ever thought of us, as God's children and looked at our children at par with ourselves and our heavenly father?

Our duty as parents is to bring up our children as responsible and God-fearing citizens and in that process, it may so happen that our children in certain situations may not be happy. Compare this situation in our relation to our Almighty Father.

God punishes those whom he loves, and everything works for good to them whom he loves. If we bear this in mind and accept these two truths, we can be sure that our grievances and difficulties will turn out as evidences of God's love to us.

Wise Solomon points out "He who spares the rod hates his son and he who loves him is careful to discipline him" (Proverbs 13:24).

A father on seeing his son chained and paraded through the streets cried in agony, admitted that he only is responsible for this and laments that, had he brought him up giving punishment at the right time for his ill deeds, this would not have happened. Is there not some truth in 'his' words?

At a time when, even caning children is a criminal offence, let us leave our children to God, pray earnestly for them, try to give good advice in deeds and words. Also, like David seek God's help in all matters concerning our children.

David inquired of the Lord "Shall I go and attack the Philistines?" Will you hand them over to me? The Lord answered him, "Go, for I will surely hand the Philistines to you" (2 Samuel 5:19). And David defeated the Philistines. Our Bible always exhorts God's children to seek God before executing our plans.

We must accept the fact that God sends trials to test our faith. God has his own plans for each one of us. Not a hair falls on the ground without his knowledge. Be strong in the Lord and in the power of his might. In that case worry and anxiety have no place in our lives.

Dear friends! Let us remember our forefathers who sacrificed themselves holding on to their faith. Hold fast, the buckler of faith. Automatically we will get the power and courage to pull ourselves up. Take courage from David's words "Even though I walk through the valley of the shadow of death, I will fear no evil, for you are with me; your rod and your staff they comfort me" - Psalms 23:4

❖ 96 ❖

He did what was right in the eyes of the Lord, but not whole heartedly.

2 Chronicles 25:2

Here 'He' refers to king Amaziah who ruled Jerusalem for 29 long years. He ruled his kingdom well pleasing to the Lord and the people. But he did not do whole heartedly. The lack of courage to make firm decisions which we see around us in many bureaucrats. In other words, Amaziah did not have the courage to do, what he believed right, with a firm hand. This halfhearted execution of his duties, was of course not good in the sight of the Lord. To do God's will is the duty of every believer whether a third party agrees with it or not. In the epistle of James it is stated that a double minded man is unstable in all what he does (James 1:8). Such an individual will be a failure in all spheres of life. To a believer in Christ this is a very pertinent question. The Bible says in Isaiah, "You will keep in perfect peace him whose mind is steadfast (26-3). Seek and you will receive is applicable only to those who seek him in right earnest. "When he asks, he must believe and not doubt, because "he who doubts is like a wave of the sea blown and tossed by the wind" (James 1:6). "That man should not think he will receive anything from the Lord" (vs.7).

Look at what our Lord Jesus Christ had said to Martha "If you believed you would see the glory of God" (John 11:40).

Our courage and the right commitment come to light when all doors are shut against us and we are tossed around. It is here that our strong faith in our Lord comes handy to make us go forward in full spirit and strength. Look how the eagles save their young birds from falling by bearing them on their strong wings. It is strong faith that our Lord Almighty will bear us in his arms, transforms us to a strong and single-minded person, to stand firm for good and the Godly ways which we strongly believe.

Dear brother! It is a strong and straight forward route that our Lord expects from us, rather than an escapist mentality. Let our Jesus Christ be our role model. With courage let us say "With your help I can advance against a troop, with my God I can scale a wall" - Psalm 18:29.

❖ 97 ❖

We can certainly do it.

Numbers 13:30

The key thought given here is the reaction of a group leader Caleb who was entrusted with the duty to explore the land of Canaan. There was another group who had an entirely different view – poles apart – of the people of Canaan. Caleb believed in God and his strength and naturally his view was based on his trust in God. Caleb said "We should go up and take possession of the land "(vs.30) whereas the other group forgetting their history (How the Lord made them go past the red sea) thought of them as insignificant compared to the size and strength of the Canaanites.

We find Caleb standing firm in his faith that they will be able to defeat the giants there and exhorted his followers to be confident and strong. Caleb had to face stoning by his followers for his confidence and courageous outlook to go to possess the land. We read of God appearing to Caleb and encouraging him; and Caleb against the resistance of others, moves along as guided by God reached the destination, the land of Canaan.

Later, we find the other group punished for spreading false reports (Numbers 14:37-38).

Dear friend! In our life's sojourn, when we come across oppositions beyond our expectations, let us think of our great God who has led us through 'red sea' situations and take courage and hold tightly to his hands.

Firmly believe "that they who are with us are much more than those who are against us" in our day to day life.

Pray to God individually thus, "Deliver me from my enemies, O God; protect me from those who rise up against me" – Psalm 59:1.

❖ 98 ❖

You did not choose me, but I chose you and appointed you to go and bear fruit – fruit that will last.

John 15:16

Jesus meeting the disciples on the night he was betrayed by Judas, had a very lengthy conversation with them. He tells them, "My command is this; love each other as I have loved you (vs.12). You are my friends, if you do what I command" (vs.14).

He went on to speak about the wine and the branches and how the branch of the vine when connected to the main stem of the grape vine, can only bring forth delicious grapes. Jesus adds "I am the vine and you are the branches, if a man remains in me and I in him, he will bear much fruit" (vs.5). Jesus here conveys to them the fact that there should be constant and continuous close relation with Jesus. He also exhorts "If you obey my commands, you will remain in my love, just as I have obeyed by Father's commands and remain in his love" (vs.10) and reminds that only in that case can they do worthwhile and fruitful service to God. And will then be deserved to be called his disciples.

Jesus Christ, our Lord conveys to us the same message he had given to his disciples and he has chosen us to do his service effectively putting our heart and soul into it, like a useful fruit bearing branch. "If a man remains in me and I in him, he will bear much fruit" (vs.5). When Christ abides in us, we get the fruit of the spirit. "The fruit of the spirit is love, joy, peace, patience, kindness, goodness, faithfulness, gentleness and self-control" (Galatians 5:22).

Dear friend! God has chosen you and me. Let us join hands and pray for God's grace to bear fruitful service to him. "Let us love one another, for love comes from God. Everyone who loves has been born of God and knows God. Whoever does not love does not know God, because God is love" - 1 John 4:7, 8.

❖ 99 ❖

I will lie down and sleep in peace, for you alone, O Lord make me dwell in safety.

Psalm 4:8

Brethren how many of us can say with confidence that we can sleep in the night peacefully? Is this not a difficult question?

Let me cite an incident that happened in the case of a couple Mrs. and Mr. Christiana Wales of Minnesota State of USA. On an extremely chilly day when the couple were stranded in their apartment due to heavy snowfall, they wondered how they could manage their dinner. They had nothing except some potatoes which Mrs. Wales boiled and served on the table. They both enjoyed eating boiled potatoes giving thanks to God the Almighty. As there was absolutely no chance of going out to buy provisions for their next meal, they together prayed earnestly to God to help them find a way. Then they heard someone knocking at their door. They opened the door and found their neighbor inviting them to have dinner with him. With a heart full of thanks, they accepted his invitation thanking God. Look, how unbelievable is this incident. But know for sure, that is how God cares for his children.

"I tossed around in the bed last night and could not get any sleep, the whole night" is a chorus we often hear in the morning from many. Contrary to this, note what the Psalmist says. "I will lie down and sleep in peace". Again we find Peter in prison, chained and in the midst of soldiers could sleep well (Acts 12:6). What else is the secret of this, except the strength of his hope and faith in God as pointed out by David. "Lord make me dwell in safety" (Psalm 4:8).

Dear friend, believe that our Lord Jesus Christ will keep us safe and sound, as has been done with our forefathers. Hold on to God with full faith like Mrs. and Mr. Wales in the true story narrated above and then we can also lie and sleep in peace and dwell in safety.

"O for a faith that will not shrink
Though pressed by many a foe
That will not tremble on the brink
Of any earthly woe"   Bathurst.

❖ 100 ❖

He will do everything I want him to do.

Acts 13:22

At the request of the synagogue rulers to address the people, Paul spoke to the men of Israel and gentiles who worship God, and what he said about David, the Son of Jesse is the key message for our thought.

God expects us also to be like David. "Do everything I want to do". In other words, implicit obedience. Our forefathers did the same thing. What did Abraham do? "Take your son, your only son Issac, whom you love and go to the region of Moriah – sacrifice him there as a burnt offering" (Genesis 22:2).

Abraham started with his son and the rest is history (vs.3-13).

Moses, Joshua and many others did what the Lord commanded them. "May it be to me as you have said (Luke 1:38). Is not this what the Lord expects from each one of us. In short, the Lord is shaping our destiny as "He is the maker of all heaven and earth". It is this that the Lord has revealed to us through Jeremiah (Jeremiah 18:4). Throughout the Bible we find many instances of this path of surrender to God's will.

Let us ponder over what Isaiah points out regarding Lord's wish given in the verses given below:

Although the Lord gives you the bread of adversity and the water of affliction (Isaiah 30:20) your ears will hear a voice behind you saying, "This is the way. Walk in it" (vs.21). Apostle Paul exhorts the Romans. "Do not confirm any longer to the pattern of this world but be ye transformed by the renewing of your mind" (Romans 12.2). Hate what is evil, cling to what is good (vs.9). Do not be overcome by evil but overcome evil with good (vs.21) etc. and hold to these principles. Listen to Jesus words "If you love me you will obey what I command" (John 14:15). In other words, let us try to live according to God's will.

Dear child of God! Let us move forward in God's way. What apostle points out in Romans 12 be our guideline.

Hymn by Mosavalsalam is apt here and its meaning 1 put it thus. "Lead us ever as per your wish

>   Not my will but yours be
>   My Lord and my Father".

❖ 101 ❖

But I have had God's help to this very day and so, I stand here and testify to small and great alike.

Acts 26:22

When the Jews brought Paul before King Agrippa, shouting that he should not be left alive, he put before the King, the back ground that resulted in his coming there. The key verse here is part of Paul's address to the king.

It can be seen in the previous passages, Paul narrating to King Agrippa how he was confronted by Jesus on his way to Damascus addressing him by name Saul (vs.11-14) and what happened to him afterwards.

If we go back to his previous history, this Saul of Tarsus, destroying the Church and going from house to house, dragging men and women and putting them in prison. (Acts 8:3). And breathing out murderous threats against the Lords disciples (Acts 9:1). We find Jesus touching him (Acts 9:4-16) and he became a new person and began preaching in the synagogue and silenced the Jews living in Damascus by proving that Jesus is the Son of God. It was because of this that he was bound and presented before King Agrippa. With undaunted courage he testified that Jesus is the Son of God, in front of the small and the great alike.

In the Holy Bible, we find another person by name Saul, son of Kish, a Benjamite, an impressive young man without equal (I Sam. 9:2) among the Israelites. Saul was anointed King by Samuel and was only 30 years of age when he became king. He was a God fearing young man and a gentleman in word and deed.

Unfortunately, as time went on, lot of changes came into his action and behaviour. He can here be compared with the seeds that fell on the rock, which sprang up quickly and dried when the sun came up, for they had no root. We find vast changes in the character of King Saul. When people shouted, "Saul has slain his thousands and David has tens of thousands", he became very angry and we read "from that time on, Saul kept a jealous eye on David" (chap. 18, vs.9). As time passed, Saul got engaged in more and more Satanic thoughts and deeds. He even sent his men to David's house to kill him (chapter 19; vs.11). Unfortunately, he had a tragic end to his life (chapter 31, vs.5)

Dear friend! It is time for us to examine in which category among these two is our place. If we are in King Saul's category, we have still plenty of time to repent and turn back to God. Take it for sure, our Lord will accept us with folded hands. If we are grouped with Saul of Tarsus, let us go ahead with the tasks entrusted to us during trials and tribulations. God the Almighty will endow us with his grace, to move forward courageously pray.

"Help me, dear Lord, to be honest and true.
In all that I say and all that I do:
Give me the courage to do what is right,
To bring to the world a glimpse of your light"   Fasick.